Writing is one of those remarkable passions where an author is privileged to enter emotional experiences that enable personal discovery. I have written since I was a little girl, exploring the relationships of family life, the complexities of growing up in a post-war Hungarian refugee family, the dramas of a wider world.

I often write about the people I love, the events that have touched me, my past and my present. My children and my family have always been and continue to be an important reason for my writing. I so greatly want them to make sense of the world, which at times is difficult and confusing. I want them to find inspiration and fulfillment and discover that the world is wonderful.

"Butterflies" has been a personal journey of discovery where I entered into the lives of burn survivors and found humor, courage and hope. This is what I want those who read my books to discover themselves. That is why I write.

Susanne Gervay

Butterflies

SUSANNE GERVAY

Special thanks is given to Dr. Hugh Martin for the time he generously donated in assisting with the medical advice in the writing of "Butterflies." Special thanks is also given to the remarkable doctors and staff of The Burn Unit, The Children's Hospital, Westmead, NSW.

While all characters who inhabit "Butterflies" are fictional, the inspiration for "Butterflies" is the courage of all those who have passed "through the fire."

First American Edition 2011
Kane Miller, A Division of EDC Publishing

For information contact:
Kane Miller, A Division of EDC Publishing
PO Box 470663
Tulsa, OK 74147-0663
www.kanemiller.com
www.edcpub.com
www.usbornebooksandmore.com

Cover design: Kat Godard, DraDog

Library of Congress Control Number: 2010941662

Printed in the United States of America
5 6 7 8 9 10 11 12 13 14 15

ISBN: 978-1-61067-043-2

Butterflies

SUSANNE GERVAY

Kane Miller
A DIVISION OF EDC PUBLISHING

Like butterflies, those who survive burns
defy their fragility to migrate large distances
and find warm climates. "Butterflies" was
written for all those heroes who survive burns
and for all those special people who help them
on their great journey.

Chapter One

"Jessie, don't you just think Mr. Roberts is the best English teacher?"

"If you say so, Katherine. It's so hot I really don't care." She slings her school bag over her shoulder. "This bag is heavy. I've got so much homework to do tonight."

"We all do. Can you stop complaining?"

"I'm not, but it's stinking weather, and I've got a ton of homework."

"Are you going to the Horror Festival, Jessie? The original *Dracula* is showing this Saturday."

"I saw 'Frankenstein' last week. Pretty good for an old movie. I'll go and see it, if I finish my 'Romeo and Juliet' homework. I hate Mr. Roberts. He gives so much work."

"I like the way he reads 'Romeo and Juliet.' 'But soft! What light through yonder window breaks? / It is the East, and Juliet is the sun.'"

"Well, I don't." Jessie smiles suspiciously at Katherine. "Is it Mr. Roberts or 'Romeo and Juliet' you're so interested in?"

"That's not worth an answer, Jessie," Katherine laughs.

The usual group of senior boys waits at the bus stop. They've got their shirts half-unbuttoned and their ties undone. It's been a hot February. Two weeks of heat wave conditions and the temperature is still a hundred degrees. Sweat drips off Marc's forehead as he clowns around, pulling out William's shirt, kicking a few bags, telling disgusting jokes.

Jessie likes Greg, the tall, skinny, redhead one standing next to Marc. Katherine elbows her. "It's him."

"Shush." Jessie gives her that "don't you dare say anything" stare.

"Girls … girls coming," Marc calls out. "What do you call ten girls standing ear to ear?" There are snickers. "A wind tunnel."

"You're the wind tunnel, if you ask me," someone calls out, but it doesn't stop Marc. The heat, the end of the school day, his mates laughing, egg Marc on.

Katherine trips over Jessie's bag as she drops it. "Sorry."

Marc mocks. "Can't keep on your feet." He stares at her. "Look, it's Dracula," he laughs. "You'll have to hide yourself in a paper bag if you want love at first bite." Marc smiles at his

2

cleverness. Some of his mates laugh.

Katherine looks up at him, her face flushed. Jessie grabs her arm. "Why don't you shut up, you idiot," she yells at Marc. "Who'd even bite you? Not Dracula, that's for sure. He wouldn't want blood poisoning."

There's sniggering. Jessie whispers, "Don't worry about him, Katherine." As the bus pulls in, she says aloud, "Marc's a pain in the neck."

Everyone laughs.

Contemptuously, Jessie taunts him. "Why don't you get a life, Marc?"

"Sure thing, as if you'd know what a life is." Marc reddens as he runs his hand through his hair.

"It's all right," Katherine lies. "I don't care." The hot air makes the eucalyptus crinkle and crack in the summer heat. She glances at the trees through the bus windows. *I've got to pretend, pretend, pretend.* Suddenly, she looks away from the cracking leaves with their broken skin. *Why did he say that? Think that? What have I done to you, Marc? I was happy today.* She watches him slouch into a sticky bus seat, sweating humidity and male scent. *I'm not going to cry. I won't give you the satisfaction.* "Yeah, why don't you get a life?"

Marc looks at Katherine quickly, pulls off his tie, then turns to discuss football results with his mates.

Jessie sits next to Katherine in a back seat. "Don't worry about him, Katherine." Jessie points to her neck. "Anyway, look." She touches a small scar just above her collar bone. "I've got this."

Katherine stares at the small scar with its fine line. She rubs sweat from her eyes and turns away. "It's so humid, Jessie. They say there'll be storms tonight. Can you study in this heat?"

"I've got to study." Jessie reverts to complaining about school subjects, teachers and exams. Katherine half-listens as she watches the boys occasionally punch each other, occasionally look around at the girls, leering and joking. She stares at their thick black shoes scuffed with kicking and tripping each other, then she kicks the seat in front of her.

The bus stops. Katherine steps out onto the sizzling sidewalk. She waves to her friends, then runs from the bus towards home, sweat dripping down her shirt into the small of her back.

She unlocks the front door. On the kitchen counter are the breakfast plates left with the remnants of toast and jam. Black ants are crawling between the strawberry jam and melted butter. *Suppose I'd better clean it up before Mum gets back.* She throws her bag into her room, hitting piles of books and CDs she's left scattered on the floor. Then she goes back to the kitchen.

The sink. Cold water first. *Cold, then hot.* The words are habitual, repetitive, persistent. The cold is a relief. Slowly, carefully, she turns on the hot water, letting it flow gradually into the cold until the sink is full. Suds slosh as she rubs and swishes plates and knives and spoons into a bubble bath of reflections. *Hide in a paper bag. Hide. Hide.* She stops, rubbing her sudsy hand along the right side of her face, down her neck, her arms, feeling the ripples of taut skin. She's heard the story so many times that she isn't sure if it is her memory or theirs.

Katherine is nearly three. Chubby and brown-eyed. There are photographs of her then. She's pretty. Mum is so young. Katherine's playing with her big sister Rachel on the front lawn outside the apartments. The oleander trees are pink. She loves the pink flowers, but they're dangerous. People get allergies from those trees, blow up with rashes and welts.

Right next to the oleanders, there is a brick pit.

Shuddering, Katherine shakes her head. She dries the plates, stacking them inside the cupboard. She goes to her bedroom, shoves clothes and mess to one side, then puts on music. Hard rock blasts through her room and between her books. Hard rock blasts into the house, blasting so that no one can hear her crying, softly at first, then louder. Louder.

"Turn down that noise!" her mother shouts, as she drops shopping bags onto the table. "Katherine, it is too noisy. Put the music lower."

Her sister, Rachel, carrying more bags, follows their mother into the house. She groans at her sister's music.

Turning down the volume, Katherine calls out, "You're so boring, Rachel."

"You're in a rotten mood."

Katherine's long hair hangs over her face so they can't see she's been crying. "I'm not. Haven't you heard of good music?"

Rachel rolls her eyes. "Right. Whatever I listen to, at least it isn't hard rock. Really bad hard rock."

"Bad? As if you'd know."

"Will you two stop fighting and help me get dinner ready?" They don't stop, and they don't help. "That is it. These marshmallows are going to hit you girls in a *momento*." They ignore her until … *plop*. Marshmallows soar into the air. One just misses Katherine. Two hit Rachel on her head. They stop fighting. Their mother is laughing. "*Bene, bene.* You look like fish with their mouths open." Her slight Italian accent makes the words sound like laughter. "Do not worry, you can still eat the marshmallows, they are not damaged. Now, come and help or there will be no food. Look what I bought for you two. Your favorite – mangoes, very sweet."

Katherine is quiet as she unpacks the groceries while her mother and Rachel gossip and prepare dinner.

"Hope you're all hungry," Rachel brings the pasta to the table. "Dinner's ready."

Their mother smiles as she slides the serving spoons into the salad. "Old Mr. Jones does love his salad, especially with the baby tomatoes. You know he has a very strong grip. At his lunch, he held on to his fork, stabbing the tomatoes. One landed on his cushion and when he lay back – squash." She's laughing now. "Tomato sauce."

"Mum, you're funny." Rachel bites into a tomato.

"That is what they say at work too." She stops laughing. "I like looking after the people in that community house. I wish for a permanent job there." She fiddles with her coffee cup.

"Who else would do that job? Who'd want to work in that crazy place?"

"It is not crazy, Katherine. I do not like you saying that. The people there need help, and I need the work."

"Those people want to be there, want to be helpless, sick." Katherine pushes away her dinner. *Not like me.*

"They are not sick. You know that. They need a little help for a while." Her mother puts down her coffee cup. "Are you all right?"

"Mum, she's just having one of her scenes. Why don't you grow up, Katherine? You're ruining dinner."

"Well, I'm so sorry."

"Stop it, Katherine." Her mother looks at her daughter. "Is everything all right? Was it school? Did something happen?"

"No." *Yes.*

Her mother waits. Watches her. Puts her hand on Katherine's arm.

Don't touch me. I don't want to be touched. But Katherine doesn't pull her arm away.

Rachel stops eating. Katherine looks away from them, confronting the kangaroo paw with its furry pods. *What are you pointing at, you stupid plant? There's nothing to point at.*

Can't I be in a bad mood if I feel like it? Stop staring, Mum. Stop staring, Rachel. You're staring a hole into me. Are you all going to just watch me? Are you afraid that if you stop looking at me, someone'll take me? You're wrong. Wrong. No one wants me. No one will ever want me. That's what he said. In front of everyone. I've got to hide. Do you want to hear that? She glares at them. *All right then, I'll tell you. A plain brown paper bag, that people stuff their leftovers in, then put in the garbage. That's what I am.* She holds her stomach as if she's going to be sick. Then shakes her head. *No. No, I can't tell.* "There's a lot of pressure from schoolwork. It's getting to me, that's all."

"You are better off than the people in the community house."

I don't need a lecture, Mum. I can't make it, if you lecture me. Not today. Please, Mum. Katherine gets up.

"Katherine. You do know you are lucky?"

Lucky, lucky me. Katherine shrugs. "Yes." *I want to go now. Let me go.* Katherine stands, looking down at her mother.

"Katherine, you have choices. Many of the people in the community house have not such choices."

You try, don't you, Mum? "You're right, Mum." *I don't want to argue today. It's hot and it's too hard. I hear what you're saying, but I just want to look normal, like everyone else, that's all.* "I've got to study."

"You've always got an excuse for not clearing up," Rachel complains.

"Your sister has to study if she wants to make the

university."

Rachel rolls her eyes.

"It is only until the end of next year." Their mother wipes down the table.

Katherine disappears into her room. *Studying. I hate it. What's the point of reading and rereading the same notes. Memorizing things I already know. There are so many other things to learn in this world. I don't understand why …* Scribbling on a note pad, she gets her pen to work. She flips open her math textbook. *Why? Scribbly little numbers. I want to scratch you out.* Dark blue lines cross and recross the notepad until Katherine's fingers hurt, and the paper is torn with holes and pen marks. *OK, OK. Calm down. Katherine, think. Think. I'm going to be a doctor. Focus. A doctor. That's the reason. Then all this'll make sense. I just need to breathe deeply, control myself. I know. I'll put on some music.* She shifts through her CDs, leaving the hard rock aside. She finds the shiny silver disk. Carefully, she blows fine dust from the disk, then inserts it into the player. The deliberateness of her movements, the concentration on the physical act, is calming. Waiting for the music, she crouches on the floor next to the player with her head bent over her knees. The gentle melody sifts through the room as she slowly traces the lines of her body with the palms of her hands.

Last month, just before school started, Katherine went with

her sister to see the brick pit. They'd been there twice before: once with their mother a long time ago and once on Rachel's sixteenth birthday. It had been hard. They cried standing over the bricks, grieving as if the pit had been a grave.

Katherine and Rachel talked about going back to see the pit again a lot of times, but there were always excuses. Study, friends, the hospital. This time it was different. No excuses. Katherine was starting senior school, Rachel starting work as a dental nurse and their mother employed in the community house. Their lives were beginning to make sense.

"We have to go and see it now, don't we? Just you and me?" Katherine asked.

"Yes."

Katherine stood in her black-laced shoes on the brick edge of the pit. A rusty metal grate was welded onto the top now, but they could still peer down into it through the bars. Leaning over the pit together, they saw sunlight disappearing into a black hole.

Katherine shuddered, then defiantly shook her head. "You're not so important are you, pit?" She kicked the edges of the bricks, scratching marks into them.

"No, not important," Rachel repeated.

They both knew it was a lie.

Tears shimmered in Rachel's eyes. "Mum never blamed me, but Dad did." She wiped her face. Touching Katherine's arm softly, she took a breath. "I need to tell you here, right in front of the pit. It ... it's so hard to say, but you have to believe me. You're my sister, and I love you. I would have saved you if I could. I wanted to save you."

"I know." Katherine awkwardly put her arm around Rachel. "You're my sister, and I love you too."

"You did it, didn't you? You pushed Katherine."

"I didn't, Daddy. I didn't, Daddy." Rachel's pale cheeks go red, and tears wet her seven-year-old face.

Rachel doesn't like her Daddy's loud voice.

He grabs Rachel's head, forcing her to look past the oleanders at the bricks. Just a square in the ground. Charcoal wood and burned firelighters lie in disjointed piles inside it. The pit isn't beautiful now, with bright lights and dancing flames. There's an aluminum lamp attached to a wall near the pit. Rachel turns her head towards the lamp. The tall reddish-haired man doesn't let her look at the shiny aluminum with its silver reflections. His heavy hand pushes her head close to the pit, past the bricks. She can just make out bits of the earthen floor lying deep under the soot and ashes.

Deep inside the pit. Deep.

Katherine had been playing, grasping for the dancing flames, when she tripped. They engulfed her small arms, and she fell into the pyre of garden refuse and chemical fumes. She screamed for Rachel and Mama. The gardener ran to her. They all ran to her. But the gasoline fire burned. Acid flames covered Katherine's brown hair and her head, burning her hair, her face, her body. Acid flames covered her arms and her little body with its chubby folds and soft baby skin.

Katherine turns the page of her math textbook, relieved to leave the algebraic equations. Geometry. She likes working out the problems, making the circles complete and the geometrical lines cross and join into perfect prisms and pyramids. There are answers, solutions. There has to be a point for the pain. The awful pain. There's got to be an answer. She presses her fingers against her lips. *I know there are miracles. The Professor said there are miracles. I'll have soft skin and pretty hair one day. One day, I'll wear my hair up. I'll be like everyone else. One day.*

She looks out of her window into the backyard where her mother's parsley and the orange marigolds grow. The lawn needs mowing. Katherine focuses on two kookaburras perched on the washing line. *Laugh kookaburras, laugh. Please laugh.* It's as if the plain gray and white birds hear her. They suddenly start laughing and playing on the clothesline pegged with sheets and Rachel's white shorts. The birds laugh and laugh, until their long triangular beaks look like smiles, and their ordinary feathers sparkle. *You're beautiful. Beautiful.* Katherine touches her hair, which is long and straight now. *Thirty-seven operations. Will I ever be beautiful? Will anyone ever want me?* She forces herself to turn away from the kookaburras and focus again on her math.

The next morning, Jessie waves at Katherine as she enters the schoolyard. "'She speaks, O speak again, bright angel, for thou art / As glorious to this night …' Well, it's day, so I won't go on with that quote. I'm exhausted. I studied *Romeo and Juliet* all night. I might even get as good at it as you are." She smiles. "But I'm still not in love with Mr. Roberts."

"You're not funny." Katherine walks with Jessie towards their lockers. They talk about last night's homework and studying and the heat until Katherine says, "You know yesterday, on the bus with Marc and his mates?"

"Don't bother about them. They're stupid, that's all."

"Jessie, listen. I have to bother about them … and about other things." Jessie looks at Katherine. "We've been friends for a long time." Katherine waits for a moment. "Are we good friends?"

"Of course we are."

Katherine lifts her hair exposing the scars, exposing her neck and her shoulder. "Can you see that?"

"Yes." Jessie shifts uncomfortably.

"Is it the same as the scar above your collarbone?" Katherine touches Jessie's small scar, making her jump backwards. "Is it thick and rough and hard in places and grafted with new skin again and again?" Katherine's brown eyes challenge Jessie. "Did you get third degree burns on half of your body?" Shivering, she speaks deliberately, slowly. "And the surgery and vomiting afterwards and the pain and no father and your mother crying with you?"

"No," Jessie whispers.

"Girl who has to hide. Girl who no one will love. That hurt. A lot. But it was worse when you compared what I've been through with your tiny scar."

"I didn't mean it. I just wanted to make you feel better."

"It made me feel like nothing. I may be ugly, but at least I don't want what I've been through trivialized. Then I'm really nothing."

"It's not trivial. I admire you. You're smart, and you *are* pretty, Katherine."

"Sure I am. Pretty as a princess." Katherine rubs her hands. "Marc and his friends laughed at me." Tears edge into the corners of her eyes. "I want to look like you. I want your little scar to be mine. I want a father to take care of us and my mother not to work so hard and the scars to disappear so I'm like you."

"Don't be like me, Katherine." Jessie bites her lip. "I didn't think. I don't know anything. I'm sorry."

"I want to be a kookaburra."

"What?"

"A kookaburra." Katherine wipes the palms of her hands. "It doesn't matter."

"I'm really sorry. You're my friend. I never want to hurt you. Please. Please."

Katherine nods.

Chapter Two

Rachel fiddles with her sister's long hair. "You've got split ends. Have to cut them off."

"Not too short. Watch those scissors. Are you cutting too much?"

"I'm not. Stop moving around." Rachel pulls at a few strands. "It'll look great for the dance."

"I don't know if I'll go."

"Don't be stupid. You've been talking about it all month. And why did I make the silk braid to thread into your hair? It took me ages to do."

"You like crafts, so it wasn't such a big thing."

"That's gratitude for you. I could have made something

for myself, you know?" Rachel pushes away rising resentment. She concentrates on her sister's hair. Carefully cutting each strand, she trims, twirls, styles, before she threads the silk braid into the long braid that hangs over the side of Katherine's face. Rachel glances at the photograph that's been on the mantelpiece for as long as she can remember.

Katherine is sitting on Santa's lap holding Small Pup, her fluffy toy sheepdog. She's wearing a white cotton dress with chocolate-colored polka dots that match the color of her eyes. There's a cream satin bow in her hair. It hangs over her left ear. On the right side and along the back of her head, there is no hair.

In the hospital, her mother had been furious at those other mothers who concealed their children's scars under hot sweaters or huge hats, making the children sticky and afraid. She attacked them. "Those burns are part of your babies. You have to accept the burns if you accept your babies."

As if in defiance of those mothers and the people who wanted their children to hide, she insists that Katherine wears a bow in her hair for the Santa photograph. Rachel is wearing a bow too. It's yellow.

"But Mama, I've got no hair. Everyone can see, Mama."

"Katherine, you cannot hide your scars or you will be hiding always." Mum pulls her cream jacket around her, then bends to kiss her little girl's scarred head and the side of her face without hair. Her voice quivers just a little bit. "I love every part of you. You are beautiful, Katherine. Make sure you smile for the photographer."

"I don't want to smile, Mama." Her face scrunches into a frown, and the satin bow wobbles. A big boy stares at her half-bald head, and Katherine dives at him, giving him a huge bite on his arm.

"My sister is strong," Rachel giggles, as the boy runs off to tell his mother. The boy's mother looks up to see their mother standing with her arms crossed and Katherine with no hair. She doesn't say anything, and Katherine is smiling when she goes up to Santa.

Rachel smiles, remembering Katherine taking a chomp out of the boy, and anyone else who stared at her.

"What's so funny? Have you wrecked my hair?"

"Right, as if I would." She points to the photo. "Katherine, do you remember when that picture was taken?"

"Sure."

"You were really cute. Santa nearly had a heart attack when you asked him for some hair for Christmas." They both laugh – a secret, connected laugh of growing up together. "Santa looked really stupid not knowing what to say. Mum whispered something in his ear, and then he told you that you'd have long hair one day, but not this year." Rachel's fingers tighten around the braid. "You got so angry, you know."

"But I have hair now."

Fluid pumps under Katherine's scalp, making her head wobble like a freakish growth. And then there's the cutting, the dragging of the stretched skin across her head, the draining of the fluid and

*pulling of her growing hair over her baldness. The pain is terrible.
Four years of operations. In the hospital, Katherine holds tightly
to the small, stuffed sheepdog that's been with her ever since the
accident, been with her into every operating room, and lies with
her at night in bed. Small Pup has bald spots too.*

*As the gurney moves towards the operating room, she
screams. "I'm scared. Scared. Mama, help me. Why are you
letting them take me?" She calls out again and again until the
anesthetic works, and her mother's crying at the glass doors that
separate them.*

"OK. Have a look in the mirror, Katherine."

She jumps up and runs to the bathroom. "This is great.
Great! You're definitely the best braid maker, for a dental
nurse. Ha! Ha!"

"Very funny." Rachel smiles at her sister. "You know
dental nurses can have other talents."

At lunchtime, everyone is talking about the dance. Jessie is
excited. "Katherine, remember, we've got to make the guys go
crazy when they see us. I've bought this blue satin top that'll
look fantastic."

"It'll go with your blue eyes. You look great in everything
anyway."

"I don't think so."

They gossip about music and teachers and the dance until

Katherine brings him up. "Marc. Do you think he'll be there?"

"Who cares if he is or isn't? He's an idiot."

"But what if he is?" She blushes. "All his friends heard what he said, you know, on that day. Everyone thought it was funny."

"Katherine, you can't let him or his friends stop you from doing what you want. I'll be there, and you know I'll have a rotten time without you. So, you've just got to come. So you're coming. Right?"

Katherine doesn't answer at first. Then she looks at her. "I guess I will."

The bell rings, and they go to their physics class. The summer sun beats through the open windows, and it is hot and humid. Katherine feels the tightness of her skin under her right arm. *I need another graft.* She rubs her leg, unconsciously massaging the stinging out of her thoughts. *I hate grafts. But I want to be able to move. I'm supposed to be happy about that. Moving my arm. I guess I am. I still hate grafts.*

Rachel is sitting on her sister's legs while their mother grabs the cream.

"You're not putting that on me, Mama."

"I will smack you if you do not keep still."

"The doctor said you can't smack me. It'll wreck the graft. So you can't. No, Mama."

"You keep still, Katherine."

"I don't have to. It hurts." She pulls away from her mother's

hands calling out, "Hurts. Agonia, Mama." Italian words slip
between her English as Katherine fights against her mother. "A
lot. Molto, molto."

"I know it hurts but ... "

Katherine gives Rachel a huge kick that knocks her onto the
floor.

"Stop it, Katherine. Stop it, Katherine!" Her mother reaches
for Katherine's good arm. "There is no graft here." She pulls her
daughter too hard, digging her hands into Katherine's smooth
skin, pressing too hard, unable to let go. Katherine is sobbing, but
her mother cannot let go.

"Mama, Mama, you're hurting me."

Suddenly, she releases her hold. She stands for a moment,
confused. Then she puts her arms around her daughters and starts
to cry softly. "I am very tired, bambine. I am sorry. Sorry. Sorry."

Jessie nudges Katherine as she picks up a pen. The teacher
is droning on about formulas and atomic structure. Jessie
conscientiously takes notes. She wants to be a scientist.
Katherine shifts uncomfortably. *My skin's so tight.* She traces
the graffiti of initials carved roughly into the wooden desk.
Shuddering at the roughness, she puts her notebook over the
graffiti. *What will I wear to the dance? I've got nothing to wear.*
I'll look ugly. I don't want to be ugly.

Jessie's long blonde hair is tied back into a ponytail that
flicks over her shoulders as she writes. *You're my friend, but*
you'll never really understand. To cool her neck, Jessie lifts her

ponytail, letting the air seep between her soft skin and her hair. *That'll never be me, will it?* Katherine shakes her head and tries to listen to the teacher.

At last school ends for the day. The weather is still hot, sticky, and the doorknob feels wet as Katherine unlocks the front door. She looks in the kitchen and her mother's bedroom. *Mama, where are you? Mama, come on. I want to talk to you. Please, where are you?* She knows her mother's at work. She got the job as an assistant. She'd been happy about it, and Katherine had tried to smile. "All the time that I spend in the hospitals, in the rehabilitation and burn groups with you, Katherine, it is not going to be wasted." Laughing, she'd added, "I even will be allowed to arrange the flowers. I love to do that."

Katherine bites her lip. *I wish you still pushed me in the stroller, delivering leaflets or doing odd jobs or cleaning. At least you were here for me.* Sometimes, when she was little, Katherine used to go with her to clean people's houses, scrubbing the bathtubs and stainless steel sinks of wealthy women and not-so-wealthy working mothers.

"Come on, Katherine, be a good girl. Bring me the broom. We must hurry up. I do not like leaving Rachel at home by herself." Katherine carries the broom precariously, making her mother laugh.

"You are a good girl." Her mother's black hair is swept back into a bun, the way she always wears it. Her clear olive skin,

brown eyes and lilting accent, mark her as Italian, but she's
Australian now. Wisps of hair escape as she leans over the broom
to sweep the kitchen floor before washing it. "I like doing a good
cleaning job for Louise. She is always kind to us." Mum squeezes
detergent into the bucket. "She likes you, Katherine. It is nice,
what she gave you." Katherine admires the white socks with
frilly lace at the top. "I have told her many times not to buy you
things." Mum's sweating as she mops the tiles. Katherine watches
her.

The kids at school have been teasing her about her mother.
Katherine defends her, shouting at them that Mama isn't just a
stupid cleaner. She'd kicked a big girl, making her cry.

"Why do you clean Keisha's house, Mama, and the houses of
other people? I don't like it." Her mother stops washing the floor
and turns to look at her eight-year-old daughter. "You can be
a secretary in an office, Mama. You can wear nice clothes and
drink cups of coffee and tea. You don't have to clean toilets. It's
embarrassing."

Her mother's dark eyes are ice, but what she says burns into
Katherine's mind. "Yes, I am a good secretary. I can write letters,
answer phone calls, drink coffee, but that is not what I do. I am
not embarrassed, ashamed. I will never be ashamed of cleaning
toilets. Is that what you said?" Katherine stares at the floor.
"Cleaning toilets? I clean them, and I scrub the garbage cans, and
I would clean the sidewalks if I have to. Do you understand why?
Look at me, Katherine." Her mother waits until Katherine raises
her head.

"I clean because we need the money, and because I cannot work in an office, going in every morning and working all day. Cleaning fits in, between those times you need me – when there are operations, or when I have to spread cream over you all through the day, or when the graft splits away, or when the graft works. I am there for you, Katherine."

She never asks her mother again about the cleaning, but afterwards, when her mother cleans, she takes a duster and dusts all the shelves.

Katherine looks for Rachel. "Where are you?" Rachel's room is tidy, her nightie neatly folded on her quilt. *Rachel's still at work. I'm sick of it. Everyone's gone. Unfair. Unfair. Just leave me, that's right. No one's there anymore to tell off those kids who call me ugly or Bald Eagle or Mashed Potato or some other rotten thing. You used to be there for me, Rachel. I don't want you to leave me alone at school or alone on the bus or alone at the dance. Everything's unfair.*

It's still hot, and her school clothes stick to her back. Katherine throws her school shoes into the bedroom and strips off her uniform and tosses it into the room too. She catches her reflection in her bedroom mirror and stops to stare. Her skin is tight. The smoothness of her left side merges into skin which looks like the broken leaves of dry eucalyptus trees. She presses her hands against her chest. She'd cried when she'd gotten her period and her breasts had tried to grow. Her left breast is soft. Her right side is different. She'd been fourteen when they'd transplanted tissue from her thigh to her breast, slotting it under her taut skin, but they couldn't make it perfect. Maybe they'll make it perfect one day. Slamming the bathroom door shut, she turns on the cold water.

"Hello, Katherine. We are home." Her mother arrives with Mexican takeout for dinner, and Rachel's brought home three sets of false teeth to practice her dental work. She's studying part time to be a dental technician.

Katherine is in her shorts and T-shirt. It's cooler now with the evening breeze. She stands watching them from her bedroom doorway. "You actually got the car started? That's good. Well, a miracle really."

"Hey, are you criticizing my car? It runs very well, you know." Rachel stands up straight, defending her first car. She's saved most of her pay for it. A twelve-year-old sedan. On Saturday afternoons she takes Katherine out, driving really fast over humps and potholes, and they scream together on the back roads.

"No, no, great car."

Their mother sets the table while Rachel fiddles with the sets of false teeth. "Dinner is ready, Katherine, Rachel."

Katherine walks to the table. "Smells good, Mum."

Rachel flashes the teeth. "What do you think? A full cleaning treatment or braces or a plate?" She winks at her mother.

"Put them away, Rachel," her mother shakes her hands. "Not at the dinner table."

Laughing, Katherine picks them up and mimics her mother, "Not at the dinner table."

"I have to write a report on dentures. I've written a draft already. Could you check it tonight? You're good at writing."

"Compliments get you everywhere. OK." Katherine runs her fingers over the teeth. The beef and bean burritos taste delicious. Her mother chatters about work. Rachel puts the teeth on the counter.

I'm happy. You're home now, you're home.

Chapter Three

Hairy ripples cover her like a hyena. Her bald head snarls with threatening teeth. It's the Beast. Too terrible. The Beast.

Katherine jerks her eyes open. Two-thirty in the morning. She rolls over onto her stomach, reaching for Small Pup. *I'm too old for you, Pup.* She feels his worn patches and presses him against her face. *I don't care.* Tucking Pup under her arm, she closes her eyes.

The Beast can't talk, but shrieks at the shining Prince who's dark and handsome. The Prince isn't afraid. He opens his arms and holds the Beast, caressing, soothing until the Beast no longer shrieks. "Your fur is velvet," he murmurs, putting his lips against her fur, whispering, "beauty" until the Beast purrs, and her ripples begin to disappear. Soft, brown hair flows down the Beast's shoulders, and her skin becomes pale and smooth. The Prince calls her Princess. He calls her beautiful. The Beast isn't a beast anymore. It has a name. Katherine.

Spoken words disturb Katherine's dreams like they've done for as long as she can remember. She calls out in her sleep.

Katherine doesn't speak after the accident. She used to say, "Mama. Rachey. Play with me. No. Brava. Chocolate." She sees the speech therapist, who is kind and makes her form sounds, but there aren't any words. Katherine's mother practices words with her, but she still doesn't speak. Rachel plays dolls with Katherine and talks for her sister.

Once her mother shouted at Katherine, "Speak! Speak! Say anything. You can. I know you can." Katherine garbles sounds, grunting out noises, grunting until her mother shakes her, until she holds her tightly, until her mother is crying.

Katherine's five, playing with Rachel in the playground on the swings, seesaw and climbing bars. She's climbing the metal bars, right to the top, even though it's hard to stretch to the next bar. She pulls with her right arm, and her chubby face strains with effort.

Her mother is talking to a friend on the park bench. She glances at the girls in between discussing recipes and ex-husbands. "Katherine, you're too high," she calls out.

Katherine looks down for a moment, then reaches higher. Her right hand tips the bar as she grasps for it, forcing scars to pull, scars to tear apart. Like a ball she crashes and rolls and bounces, calling out, screaming, "Mama, Mama, Mama!"

Katherine's arm is broken, but she speaks after that. The doctor says it's because of the shock. The speech therapist says she's just ready. The counselor says she learned that her mother and sister can't do everything for her. She has to talk herself.

"Hurry up, Rachel. I need a shower now. I'll be late for school."

A teasing voice trickles out of the keyhole. "You'll just have to wait. Ever heard of that?"

Katherine bangs on the bathroom door.

"Stop that noise." Their mother shakes her head as she pours herself coffee.

"Oh, Mum, by the way, I'm going shopping with Jessie after school. She's got to buy some shoes for the dance next Saturday. I haven't anything to wear. I saw something at The Fashion House. I'll use the birthday money Nonna and Grandpapa sent from Italy."

"The shower's empty," Rachel laughs.

"About time." Katherine races into the bathroom, slamming the door. The sound of gushing water and Katherine singing blare through the house.

"She never stops talking." Her mother smiles.

"I thought I wouldn't make it until lunchtime." Katherine

eats her spinach and tomato salad and olives as she and Jessie wander up the hill to their group's regular lunch spot. "I was starving in Biology. I was thinking that dissected frog looked pretty delicious."

"That's disgusting. You're obviously dieting again. Katherine, your ten-day diets, your grapefruit and egg diets, your ... what was that other diet? That's right, the Israeli Army diet. They're ridiculous. Bet you didn't have breakfast."

"Maybe I did have breakfast, maybe I didn't."

"You didn't, and you always end up scavenging my food." Other girls say hello as Katherine and Jessie sit down between them.

"I don't scavenge." Katherine looks into Jessie's lunch bag. "Can I have some of your dried apricots?" Nudging Jessie, she takes one. "Better than a green slimy frog." She eats an apricot. "Wish I could eat anything I wanted and look like you."

"You do eat anything you want. You're always stuffing yourself with my lunch." Jessie takes out her peanut butter sandwich.

"Can we not talk about dieting? Just become a vegetarian like me, and you'll be fine." Liz doesn't wait for objections and starts talking about the Horror Film Festival. "Did anyone see the last film of the Festival? 'House of Wax?' Vincent Price was brilliant as the burned sculptor. He was demented, killing people so that he could make them into waxworks."

"Definitely more interesting than apricots." Julia scrapes

her fingernails across her pencil case, making them all scream, "Stop! Stop!"

Food is forgotten as they argue and giggle over haunted houses, werewolves, Dracula, corpses rising from the dead, evil Freddy Kruger being burned. Horror movies twist and turn, weaving between apricots and olives.

Katherine shudders, trying to stop thoughts of burning Freddy and body snatchers. *Talk about something else. Anything else.* Katherine interrupts determinedly. "What's everyone think about the dance on a harbor ferry?"

Julia tries to finish her story about a vampire sucking blood, but can't compete against the dance.

"What'll I wear?"

"Who's going?"

"The harbor?"

"It'll be great. Sea breezes … It'd be too hot to have a dance at school. We'd be disgustingly sweaty." Liz finishes her apple and puts the core in her lunchbox.

"You know why it's on a ferry?" Julia smiles knowingly.

Lounging back on the grass, Jessie asks, "Why?"

"It makes it a dry party. No alcohol. I bet the teachers will frisk the guys as they board."

Jessie grins. "I'd like that job."

"Very funny. Some of those guys aren't going to like the alcohol ban."

"So what? They'll have to live with it. We're worth it, aren't we? Anyway, I'm definitely not interested in alcohol

and throwing up. Those losers were trashed last time."
Jessie looks at her sandwich. "Just the thought of vomiting
turns me off my lunch. Anyone for half a peanut butter
sandwich?"

Katherine un-tucks her shirt. It's wet with perspiration.

"Anyway, the guys will be trapped on the boat," Liz adds.

There's a musical laugh from Jessie. "With us." They giggle
about the boys and which ones they like and what's funny
about them until the bell goes.

Mr. Roberts returns the class essays on "Romeo and Juliet."
"That was excellent, Katherine." He hands her paper back.

Jessie nudges her. "'Parting is such sweet sorrow, / That I
shall not say good night till it be morrow.'"

Katherine kicks Jessie under the desk.

The bell goes, and there's the scraping and pushing of
chairs under desks and the sound of books slamming shut.
"Last class today, Katherine. Relief. Water. It's too hot."

"I've got swimming practice tomorrow morning. Wish I
was swimming tonight."

"And why did you kick me in English class? It hurt." Jessie
rubs her foot.

"As if you don't know why. And as if that hurts. Have you
thought of acting as a career?"

"All I was doing was pointing out a few things. Mr.
Roberts always pays you special attention. Mr. Roberts, Mr.
Roberts, where art thou, Mr. Roberts?"

"Yes, it's called English." Katherine tugs Jessie's ponytail.

"You're pushing it. Can we forget Mr. Roberts? Are we going shopping?"

Jessie laughs as she packs her bag. "Shopping. Shopping. We've got to sacrifice ourselves, trudging tirelessly, heroically through shops. We have to look gorgeous, hot or not."

Katherine's shaking her head. "Yes, you're definitely an actor. Forget science."

"Sure." Jessie taps her watch. "We've got serious shopping to do, and we haven't much time. Let's go. My dad gets really angry if I'm home late. I can't stand him sometimes."

"Come on, your dad's all right."

"He's not. You should hear him shout at Mum and my brother and me, especially after he's been working all day in that great and wonderful law firm. You'd think it was a prison camp, the way he goes on."

"At least you've got a dad." Katherine swings her bag over her right shoulder.

"You don't know anything about it." Jessie's voice rises. "Everything has to be exactly how he likes it. He's controlling and …"

Katherine puts her hand on Jessie's arm. "You're right. I don't know."

Jessie stops.

"We're going shopping, and you know that we love shopping."

Jessie laughs. "Shopping. You want to go to The Fashion House, don't you? Love their clothes."

"Me too."

"But shoes first."

They race for the bus. They're puffing as they scramble up the steps of the bus. Marc's at the rear with his mates. He looks up at Katherine. She quickly sits down, turning her back on him. Jessie doesn't notice him. Katherine's relieved when it's their stop, and they can get off.

"This is the tenth shoe shop we've been in, Jessie. I don't think there are any more shoes to try on."

"You're a bit dramatic. Who's the actor now?" Jessie slips on a pair of high-heeled sparkling blue shoes.

"They look great. Buy them."

"Are you just saying that to get out of here?" Jessie flicks her ponytail.

"No. Well, yes, but they do look fabulous."

"Are you sure?"

Katherine nods. "I promise. Fabulous."

"Very sure?"

"Yes. Yes. Yes."

"OK. I'll buy them." As she pays for her shoes, she looks at her watch. "There isn't much time, and we've got to get your dress." She bites her lip. "I've been a bit selfish, I think."

Katherine looks at her seriously. "You're right." Then she laughs. "Come on then, Jessie. We've got to move. Let's get to The Fashion House before it closes. Lucky for you, I know what I want."

They run all the way, panting as they fall through the door of the boutique. "Air conditioned, thank goodness." Katherine goes straight to one of the racks. She pulls out a strapless black velvet dress. "It's beautiful, isn't it?" Stroking the fabric, she shivers with anticipation. "I love velvet." She heads for the dressing room. "I hope I fit into this."

"Of course you will, even though you ate nearly all my apricots."

"As if I did," Katherine sings through the dressing room door.

The shop assistant asks Jessie how everything is going. "I'm waiting for my friend. She's looking for a dress for our dance." They wait for Katherine to emerge.

"I'm here." She swirls around, so that her long brown hair spreads out in a whirlwind.

Jessie laughs.

The shop assistant watches uncomfortably and plays with her gray leather watchband. Katherine swirls around again. The shop assistant murmurs, "There's a wide selection of dresses to choose from." She moves towards the clothes racks and carefully selects a dress. "What about this one?" she stammers. "That dress you're wearing doesn't look quite right, don't you think?" She holds out a plain black cotton frock with long, dark sleeves and white buttons right up to the neck.

Katherine reddens. Instinctively, she rubs her hands along

her scarred arms and up her neck, then stares defiantly at the shop assistant. "No. I'll take this strapless dress, thank you."

Chapter Four

"Come on, Katherine. Come on." Her mother's and sister's voices tunnel through the water, urging Katherine to swim faster, faster. *Come on. I can do it. Just push yourself, Katherine. Push. Strong strokes. Fast strokes.* She's tailing the swimmer on the right. *I only need an extra second.* There is screaming as Katherine edges towards the other club's swimmer. *I can see you. Closer ... Push, Katherine, push ... Equal ... I can do it. I can. Can. Equal ... Keep going, touch the wall, stretch, faster, stretch, stretch ...* The wall. There's cheering. Second place.

Katherine punches the air with her left arm, rips off her goggles, then takes a dive. The salt water stings her eyes. *Second place. Smile, Katherine.* She smiles, waves to her team's supporters. "That was wonderful," her mother calls out, from the edge of the sea pool. Katherine looks past her mother to the surf crashing against the rocks. Her mother's voice is insistent, forcing Katherine to turn away from the sea. "You were wonderful." *Wonderful? Am I, Mum? Second place. That's not wonderful. I don't want to be second. I can't be second if I'm going to make it.*

"It was a pretty good time," Katherine lies. She wraps a towel quickly around herself as always, avoiding the stares of strangers before she joins her teammates. The coach is preparing everyone for the relay, talking about last minute strategy and teamwork. Katherine will be the second swimmer. While she listens, she rubs the towel against her back, then under her arm. Staring at the towel, she suddenly shoves part of it behind her. When everyone's attention is on the coach, she feels under her right arm. It's sticky. The skin is broken. A tear. Her stomach knots. *I don't want this. Please. Please.* The ocean breeze is warm, and the evening air hot and steamy, but her teeth chatter. *Why do I keep trying? Why do I pretend that I can do it? Me, a winner? I'm ...* She presses her hand against her lips, forcing the trembling to stop. *I'm not like everyone else.*

The water is rough blue, smelling of salt and sea, so different from pale blue surgical walls smelling of antiseptic and gauze. *A graft. That'll mean two months out of swimming.*

The coach interrupts her thoughts. "Katherine, did you hear what I said? You've got to go out fast."

"Yes." *A graft. The hospital.* She rubs the back of her leg. *A graft will mean I'll miss the season. The practice sessions. All those mornings Rachel's driven me to the pool. She'll kill me.* But Katherine knows her sister won't kill her, and she knows something else. The scars under her arm won't stretch. Katherine looks at the coach. *I'm slower. The race.* Her right arm had pulled against the burns as she pounded the water in unbalanced strokes. *It was so hard. Freestyle. Except nothing's free for me.* She grits her teeth. *Everything costs for me. Mum says I'm lucky. I hate her saying that. I don't feel lucky.* Katherine starts breathing deeply, trying to stop the growing panic. *Calm down, calm down. I swam tonight, didn't I? I just have to swim faster next time, train harder.*

The coach walks with them to the starting blocks. "To win this race you have to focus. Focus on your stroke, turns, kicking, pacing. There shouldn't be anything else in your mind. The mind is as important as the body."

Carefully padding towards her block, Katherine stares at the gray concrete. *Focus … turn quickly, push.* Her feet drag against the gravelly bits. Ripples tingle down her back, and she shudders. She looks up. The last reds of the day stretch over the evening ocean. White manes crash onto darkening sand. *I can't focus on kicking and pushing water and gravelly concrete, Coach. But you're right. The mind is important, but it's not like you say, Coach. I don't want to focus on the way my feet drag along concrete, the way my arms splash through water. There's got to be more. When I swim, there are no concrete walls.*

I swim right through them, out into the ocean, like the dolphins.
They're so beautiful and fast. Champions. No. I won't have a
graft. Not here, not now, because I am a dolphin tonight.

Rachel, Katherine and their mother walk towards the car. Kids
wave, parents carry towels and goggles, the sound of water
drifts between onlookers and participants.

"I am very proud of you, Katherine," their mother says.
"First for the relay. Second for your own race. We will call your
nonna and grandfather. They will be so proud of you too."

Katherine nods.

There's a jerk forward as Rachel clutch-starts the car. "A
bit of a problem with the starter, that's all." Concentrating on
the gearshift, she methodically maneuvers the car through the
traffic.

Katherine watches the gearshift jerk left, right, vaguely
hears her sister's foot move between accelerator and brake,
listens to her mother mumble about service stations and
swimming. Hot air blasts through the car window, cutting
the stifling heat. Katherine's long hair flickers in the wind like
strands of sticky honey.

Rachel stops in the driveway with a satisfied grin. "Made it."

They enter the family room, which always smells of
flowers and kitchen herbs, like their nonna's stone house
clinging to the cliffs above the Ligurian Sea. Handblown
Venetian glass and a white marble figurine sit beside red

kangaroo paw in an Australian earthenware pot.

Katherine slouches on an old stuffed armchair as she reaches for the phone. "Nonna, I can't hear you. Yes ... the line is clearer now. Yes, I'm happy that I came second. My time is fast ... Yes, I'll swim for my team ..."

Then her mother takes the phone. Her soft Italian relates the events of her life in Australia, as she reconnects herself with her parents and that other life that is still part of her.

Katherine listens for a while, catching gossip about the Napolis who moved to Rome, the good weather and the huge crop of olives this season in the groves among the hills.

Three Christmases ago, when most of Katherine's hair transplants had been completed, when her hair camouflaged scars and striations, they went to Italy. Grandpapa had sent the tickets, and they'd flown for twenty-three hours, right across the world. Rome for a day. Their mother had taken them to St. Peter's Basilica. Katherine remembers wandering with her sister and mother through the baroque colonnades that opened to an expansive piazza. She'd caught her breath when she saw the magnificent Basilica, but it was Michelangelo's Pieta that made her cry. Michelangelo's statue of a mother who seemed like a girl, cradling her dying child, who was a man. *Is life like that? Does it hurt so much?* Katherine put her arm through her mother's then. Afterwards they bought one of the many copies of the Pieta from the souvenir stalls that surround the square. Their Pieta had been more expensive than the cheap imitations in plastic and bronze. Katherine selected a small white marble figurine.

They stayed a month in their grandparents' village on the northern coast, looking out towards the island of Corsica. Katherine felt she'd always known the village. When she was a little girl, before she would fall asleep, her mother would gently speak Italian and tell stories. Stories about growing up among medieval walls and castles, and pines and olive groves that descended into fishing villages of blue harbors and netted sands. Rachel listened, but somehow those stories were part of their mother and Katherine.

"Papa, my home is Australia," their mother said to her father, blushing with confusion.

That Christmas, donkeys climbing windy, narrow streets, old widows in black, beautifully dressed girls coming home from Milan, and markets filled with food and flowers, pushed Australian beaches and hot sun into another time. On Christmas day, scents of holly and mistletoe mingled with warm cooking as doughy cappelletti, hot chestnuts and lentils wafted throughout the house.

They had been part of a family with aunts and uncles, first and second and third cousins and step-cousins and grandparents. Grandpapa had sat at the head of the table.

I miss ... I want ... need ... I don't know. Something that was there in Grandpapa's house. Suddenly she thinks of her own father. Katherine's mother said that he left them after one of their terrible arguments over money and children. "I'm never coming back," he'd shouted.

Her father visited Katherine once in the hospital.

Katherine looks like a mummy with white bandages wrapped around her head and chest and leg. Rachel is sitting on the hospital bed with colored pencils and a large drawing book. Katherine grabs a blue pencil and draws a wobbly bow on Rachel's carefully colored yellow horse. "Don't," Rachel shouts, reaching for the blue pencil. "I'm telling Mama when she comes back."

"What's going on here?" a deep voice asks.

They stop and look up at a man with reddish hair in a checkered shirt, black trousers and big boots. He's carrying a box of chocolates.

Katherine's eyes light up. "I like chocolates."

Rachel's blue eyes are dark and scowling.

"How are you, Rachel and Katherine?" he asks awkwardly.

Rachel nudges her, whispering, "Don't speak to him."

"You can't tell me what to do, Rachel." Katherine smiles, and her chubby cheeks glow. "I'm good. Do you know my mama?"

"Yes." He pauses. "I've brought you chocolates." He moves closer to the bed to give her the box. "I am ..." he hesitates, then looks at his shoes. The sharp scent of male aftershave clashes with the lingering fragrance of their mother's talc and perfume.

Rachel stares determinedly at the linoleum floor. Katherine takes a caramel chocolate. He watches them for a while, then leaves before their mother returns.

"I hate him." Rachel snatches her picture of the yellow horse from the bed and sits in the corner of the room.

Katherine looks at her sister curiously, then chooses another chocolate, a hazelnut whirl. "Yummy. Do you want one, Rachel?"

"No."

Hazelnut whirls. I don't like them much. Bed is cool with newly washed white sheets that smell of clean soap. Rachel calls out, "Good night," as she turns off her light.

"Night, Rachel."

Their mother tinkers in the kitchen, clattering dishes. She calls out, "Sleep well, *bambine*." Katherine turns her bed lamp off and puts Small Pup beside her. "Night." The house is quiet, safe with her mother and sister inside. Katherine's bedroom door is shut, the room closed to intruders. She closes her eyes cautiously. *I don't want to dream. I don't want to dream,* but water splashes through her thoughts until she's swimming, endlessly trying to catch the swimmer in front.

The next morning Katherine is tired as she walks through the school gates. Jessie's standing there waiting for her. "How was the swim meet?"

"All right. Our relay team came first."

"That's great." Jessie isn't really listening. "Guess what? Guess. You can't guess."

"Probably not. You're going to tell me though, aren't you?" She drops her bag down onto the black pavement. "This is heavy."

"My bag is too." Jessie's nearly breathless. "It's Greg. He asked me to the dance. He's just the cutest, most sensitive guy, everyone knows that. Should I go with him? Should I?"

What? The dance? "Greg? What do you mean?"

"Aren't you listening? He's asked me, can you believe it? Me, to the dance."

Listening? You're going with me, aren't you? I can't go without you. Greg? Aren't you my best friend?

"Katherine." Jessie tugs Katherine's sleeve. "Are you all right?"

"Yes. Yes. Greg. That sounds like great news. You've liked him for ages." *Like him? What about me? Do you like me?*

"Well, I haven't said yes to him yet because I had to ask you if you minded. There'll be all the other girls there at the dance. You'll know everyone. Will it be all right?"

No … No, it's not all right. It's wrong. Didn't we buy your sparkling shoes together? What about my black dress? I'm scared of going without you. You know that. You said you wouldn't go without me … and Marc will be there.

"It'll be fine. I'm glad for you." *I want to go home.* "Look, I've got to get some books from the library before class this morning, so I'll see you at lunch, if that's OK?"

"Sure. You promise you don't mind about me going with Greg? It's just that if I don't go with him, he'll ask someone else. Then he'll probably never ask me out again."

"I said it's fine. I've really got to get to the library." Katherine walks quickly to the library, then past the library, up the stairs, up more stairs, up to the out-of-bounds roof area. There's only Justine there, illegally smoking against the railing. Katherine ignores her and slumps against a wall. Sliding down the rough brick face, she sits with her head bent over her lap. Rubbing her hands up her thighs, up her sides, along her arms, her neck, her head; she explores the ripples that are part of her. *You'll never leave me, will you? You come with me everywhere. Everywhere. Jessie. Jessie, I trusted you, like I trust my sister and my mother.* The bell rings.

At lunchtime, Jessie talks about Greg until everyone groans. "All right, all right. He's fantastic."

"I know you love apricots. Do you want some?" Jessie flourishes dried apricots in front of Katherine, making some of the girls laugh.

"No, thanks. I don't feel like any today." Katherine bites into her focaccia.

"Since I'm going with Greg, Katherine can go with one of you." The girls chatter, talking about where to meet Katherine before they get on the harbor cruise.

This is humiliating. What are you doing, Jessie? Why do you think you can organize my life? Just so you don't feel any guilt about letting me down? Well, feel the guilt. "Honestly, everyone, I'll be all right. I'll get there if I want to. What's everyone wearing anyway?" That's all they need for conversations to change, crisscrossing between clothes and makeup and guys.

Rachel is making dinner tonight. She's good at cooking because she's been doing it since she was a little girl. Her mother had to be with Katherine in the hospital. That's when Rachel got used to unlocking the back door with her key, taking off her school uniform, doing her homework, putting on her dinner, then watching television until her mother came home, and she felt safe to go to bed. Her mother would leave dinner packets that Rachel could just heat in the microwave oven, but later she learned to cook ravioli, lasagna, scrambled eggs, even pesto tortellini. Tonight she's making spaghetti with homemade bolognaise sauce.

"Needs a bit more basil." Rachel stirs the pot full of bubbling pasta sauce.

Katherine stands over her sister. "I've come to inspect. Looks good."

"I'll be good when you learn to make this pasta too." Rachel wrinkles her nose, making her freckles join into a question mark.

"I'll never be as good at it as you." *I should cook. It's not fair, but there's a safe feeling I get when you cook. I'll help you with your assignments instead.*

Rachel shakes her head, then taps the pot with her big ladle. "Ready or not." They sit around the table, passing parmesan cheese, pasta and sauce, pouring water into glasses, twirling spaghetti onto their forks.

Their mother puts down her fork. "I feel sorry for Jack. He is only eighteen, and no one will visit him. I talk to him. He doesn't like the community house."

"What's he there for, Mum?"

"Rehabilitation from the drugs. Young people ruin their lives. Jack is a good boy. I will take him Rache's pasta."

"You're kind, Mama. I'm lucky to have you as my mother." Katherine looks at Rachel. "And you as my sister."

Rachel laughs. "You didn't say that yesterday when I told you off about leaving a mess in the bathroom."

"It wasn't that messy."

"Forget about the bathroom. Something's happened because you're too ... what's the word? Sentimental. That's it, too sentimental."

"Nothing's happened. Can't a person appreciate her family?"

Her mother hides a smile. "Yes, that is very nice. We like being appreciated. Katherine, is there something else?"

A waft of garden scent trickles through the back door, mingling with the cooked pasta. Katherine breathes in the smells of her home. "How come friends just let you down?"

"Friends?"

Katherine twists and turns the spaghetti in her bowl.

"Leave the spaghetti alone, will you?" Rachel sprinkles parmesan cheese onto her plate. "So are you going to tell us?"

"Maybe. I don't know."

"Well, get on with it."

Katherine hesitates. "Nothing's happened. It's just that I've got so much studying and practicing to do, I haven't got time for the dance. I didn't want to go. It was Jessie's idea."

"But you've bought a dress for it," Rachel interrupts, "and what about the braid I made for your hair?"

"I love the braid. I'll wear it some other time. It doesn't mean I have to go to the dance just because of it. I needed a dress anyway." Her voice peters out. *I can't go. I can't. Who'd want to dance with me? No one. Jessie'll be with Greg. I'll stand alone in a corner, and everyone will dance or talk, except me. What can I talk about anyway? Grafts? Operations? My scars? My hair? I want to wear my hair up. Why can't I even do that? I'm not going to the dance. Marc'll be there for sure. What if he calls me something awful? What if he says I should hide in a paper bag again, in front of everyone? That's me, girl who has to hide. I want to go to my room.* "Jessie's found someone else she wants to be with at the dance. Greg."

Her mother pushes aside her bowl, then looks up at her daughter. "Katherine, I want you go to the dance."

I'm scared. Really scared. Please, Mum. You don't understand. You can't even see what I really look like. "Mum. No."

"Is it because Jessie is with this Greg?"

"No," Katherine lies, "but she isn't much of a friend, is she?"

"I do not know that."

Katherine shrugs.

"I think you should be there with your school." Her mother speaks softly. "Do you want to run away? If you do, then you will always have to run. I do not want that for you."

I don't either, Mama. But I can't go. "I'm not running away, Mum."

"Please, Katherine, promise to think about it. I would like you to go."

Katherine nods that she'll think about it, then gets up from the table and takes her plates to the sink.

Chapter Five

The Beast is swimming in the blue sea, pushing, struggling against whirlpools of water, sucking her downwards. Rachel is driving her beaten-up car along the sand, calling out, "Where are you? Where?"

Flicking her ponytail in the air, Jessie's dancing in her new shoes, heels so high she looks fifteen feet tall.

"I'm here. Here. Can't you see me?" Her mother skips by, ignoring Katherine screaming out for her. Her mother keeps skipping as the Beast screams, drowning in water, choking in water, gasping, "Hiding girl ... hiding girl ... hiding girl."

"Please. Please help me," Katherine murmurs in her sleep, rustling sheets, stretching out her arms.

"I don't want to go on this harbor cruise. I shouldn't have said yes." Katherine's voice rises in increasing panic. "Where's Mum? How do I look?"

"Mum's finishing the laundry." Rachel puts down her magazine. "How do I know what you look like? I can't see you. Come out of the bedroom, and I'll do a few last-minute touches to your makeup."

"No one can fix me. I can't go. You can't force me to go. Mum can't either." Katherine flings herself onto her bed, but she leaves her door open, signaling to Rachel that she can come in.

Rachel wanders into her sister's room with a comb and makeup. "That dress is great on you."

"You can see my burns. My hair doesn't cover my shoulders." Katherine rolls onto her back, holding her stomach. "I shouldn't have bought this dress. And I look ugly and fat."

"You're a fathead, if you ask me." Rachel takes her hand, pulling her up. "And you're wrong, the dress looks just right. I wouldn't say it if I didn't mean it. You're scared, that's all."

"No, I'm not."

"Let me fix the braid in your hair. You always let me."

"Well, I'm not a little girl anymore, Rachel. No."

"You're acting like one."

Katherine breathes quickly, trying to control her panic.

"All right, if it makes you feel better. And I'm not scared."
She turns away from Rachel to face the open window. The
temperatures have been dropping with the cool southerly
breezes. Rachel rustles the ends of her sister's hair, then gives
her a lipstick.

Kookaburras. They're perched contentedly on the
clothesline, not caring that there is laundry to be hung or
drama inside the house. Katherine starts when they suddenly
flap into the trees, disturbing a plain brown butterfly. Then
she notices her mother carrying her wicker basket. Her
mother is wearing her laundry blouse, stained with bleach
and scrubbing. It's calming, watching her mother bend to pull
sheets and towels from the wicker basket – pegging, bending,
pulling, pegging, enjoying the breeze as she completes her
familiar cycle. For a moment, her mother stops to watch the
butterfly land softly on a white sheet. Katherine watches the
butterfly too.

Katherine half-listens to Rachel's chatter about her
technician's course, her work, and promises that she'll have
a great time at the dance. The brown butterfly leaves the
white sheet to flitter through the garden of marigolds and
sweet-smelling jasmine. *Brown butterfly, brown butterfly, you're
protected tonight in my mother's garden. Am I protected too?*

*Swollen eyelids shut tight. Head shaved bare. The woman strokes
the baby's face. A seven-year-old girl holds onto the woman's skirt.
A plastic tube feeds into the baby's nose and a drip is taped onto*

her arm. A catheter empties urine into a bag. Her arms are in splints. Her small body wrapped in gauze. Her hands are in mittens also tied to splints. She tries to open her eyes, searching through the swelling.

The nurse comes to check tubes and vital signs.

The woman brushes back her dark wispy hair and looks up at the nurse. "What is wrong with that baby? Where is her hair? Her face? Her body?"

"Remember the doctor spoke to you about it?" The nurse's voice gently persists. "Remember? Remember?"

"No. Spoke to me? No."

"About her body, her face." Pulling a chair close, the nurse sits next to her. "The baby will ... she will ... look a little different."

The woman stares, confused at the nurse in her white uniform. "Where is Katherine? Where is my baby? My little girl?"

The nurse answers softly. "This is Katherine. You can see her."

"But I can't. I can't ... see her. I can't see her."

"Katherine, are you ready?" her mother calls, as she comes into the house. She stops when she sees her daughter with her long brown hair flowing and the warmth of black velvet embracing her. "You look beautiful."

"That's what mothers are supposed to say."

"You are my beautiful daughter tonight."

Katherine shrugs, but inside, her stomach knots. "All right, Mum."

Rachel calls, "Katherine, you'll miss the boat."

Katherine shakes her head.

Her mother sits in the front seat beside Rachel. "I have saved nearly enough for a new car."

"Don't you like mine, Mum?" asks Rachel. The car starts with only three turns of the ignition. "No one can say that this car isn't the best now, can they?"

Rachel drives through dimly lit back streets, over speed bumps that make the car sound like it's falling apart, until she reaches their favorite route. Winding alongside the national park, summer has brought color to the gray-greens of the bush. Red-pronged banksias, soft yellow wattle buds, fluffs of white gum flowers, flicker between headlights and the last rays of sun. Katherine watches the eucalyptus trees, vaguely listening to her mother talk to Rachel about a movie they're seeing tonight.

Rachel reaches the freeway. There is no conversation now as she concentrates on joining the stream of cars, turning onto the freeway and putting her foot on the accelerator. The radio hums an old Beatles tune as they head for the quay, settling into the rhythm of the car's spinning wheels.

Finally, Rachel pulls up alongside the curb. "We're here."

"You had better go, Katherine. You must not be late. Do not worry, we will be here at eleven to get you."

Katherine slides out of the back seat, stands beside the car, straightens her dress, touches her hair, looks around, waits, straightens her dress again, rubs her hands along her panty hose, looks around …

Rachel calls out of the window, "Are you going or not? We'll be late for the movies, you know."

"You won't be late. I've just got to get my dress straight."

"It is straight." Rachel waves her away. "And I put your camera in your bag. You nearly forgot it."

"You look lovely. Just go now, Katherine."

Katherine reluctantly walks across the road towards the promenade, leaving her sister and mother watching her. Street buskers playing guitars, open-air cafes, the lights of the harbor, create an excitement. Katherine shakes her head. *I'm going to have a good time. I am. I'm sick of being scared.* Katherine sees her friends at the ticket stand. She takes a deep breath, then runs to join them.

"Hi, everyone. You all look fantastic. Love your bag, Liz."

"Made from vinyl, not leather."

"We all love animals, but no lectures today," Julia interrupts.

"There's William." Katherine glances at him, then looks away.

"Mr. Roberts is over there. He's one of the chaperones tonight." Liz thinks that's funny.

"He's wearing an earring. Can you believe it?"

"Have you got your camera?"

The talk moves between dresses and guys and insecurities as the girls board the ferry.

The lights of the city sparkle as the ferry heads out into the harbor. The lights inside the boat are dimmed, the band loud, the dance floor empty, as groups of girls and boys settle into opposing corners of the boat. A few couples edge towards the floor, moving in time with the beat, but they don't dare dance yet. The girls giggle and start to move to the music until one of them pulls another, who pulls another, who pulls another … who pulls Katherine uncertainly onto the floor, until they're all jumping around, circling, partying. Jessie sees Katherine and joins her on the dance floor, dragging Greg with her. The first male. A sign that the boys in the corners can join the dancing and start partying seriously.

The band takes a break. Girls hang around the drummer and guitarist. A few boys drool around the lead singer who's wearing a black leather bodysuit and a diamond stud in her nose. The buildup of sweat and body heat from the dance floor eases with the break, as people retreat onto the decks.

"Come on, Katherine. Let's go and fix our makeup." Jessie looks at Greg. "Be back soon." They push their way through the crowds for serious discussion. Jessie can hardly wait until they're in the bathroom. "He's so nice, Katherine. I guess I let you down, but you'll just have to forgive me because Greg is … I can't explain it. Don't you think he's got the most gorgeous green eyes? Pale green, so romantic, and he's so tall. He plays in the top team for football as well as basketball. We can go watch him next Saturday. He's got some really good-looking friends you might like. Carlo, Jimmie, Reuban. What do you think?"

"I think you've lost it. Your brain, that is." Katherine

half-laughs. *And you don't deserve it, but I forgive you.*

"What do you really think about Greg?"

"He seems nice, but I don't know him yet."

Other girls move around the mirrors, adjusting skirts, smoothing on lipstick, combing hair before they leave the security of closed doors and girlfriends for another onslaught outside. One girl reports excitedly, "Some of the guys have flasks. They're drinking on the top deck. Marc's there. Do you want to go up?"

Katherine bites her lip. *Now I know where not to go.*

"Who cares about Marc and those losers?" Jessie checks her makeup in the mirror.

"Not me," Katherine snaps. She stares at her reflection in the mirror. *Not me. Not me. Girl who has to hide. I'm not going to the deck, not because of you, Marc. I don't want to hide up there sneaking sips from a flask. It's pathetic. I don't care what you think. You're … unimportant to my life. Unimportant.* Slowly, she brushes her hair, careful to camouflage her neck and shoulder. She takes Rachel's lip gloss out and smoothes it over her lips. *This is my night with my friends. They accept me, and I am what I am, at least tonight. I've seen a few frogs on the ferry, Marc, and guess what? You're not even a frog. You're a big, ugly, croaky toad. I don't like toads.* Katherine smiles. *And you never know, there might even be a prince out there for me.*

Jessie and Katherine go back to the dance floor. Greg's waiting for Jessie. "Do you want to go onto the deck and see the ocean?" He takes her hand.

Katherine winks. "There're a lot of stars tonight." Voices from the dance floor call out for her. "In a minute, I'm coming." She rummages in her bag, takes out a camera. "One photo. Smile, Jessie, Greg." She leaves them standing together as she moves onto the dance floor, her camera flashing as she takes photos of the band, her friends, some of the boys, a photo of Mr. Roberts, who's dancing with the head of English.

It's late by the time the heat and energy disperse the crowd. A few escape to the cooler air of the decks. Others lean against the bar with its *No Alcohol* signs or sit at packed tables. Katherine dances next to Julia and Liz until Julia leaves with a short guy to get drinks. The music becomes faster, and Liz joins a circle of wild ones. Katherine doesn't know how she ends up dancing with William. His movements aren't quite coordinated, and he steps out of tune to the drummer's beat. He talks about going north to surf after his exams. *I love the sea.* "Then I want to go to college. I'd like to teach." She stares at him for a moment, then bends her head. *You've got hazel eyes. Hazel like kookaburras' feathers.*

They dance and dance, joining Liz's group for a while, separating when he gets her a water, dancing closely as the music slows, discoing apart when it's wild. The beat is hectic when Mr. Roberts bumps into Katherine. "What noise is this? Ho!"

"Mr. Roberts, we're not in English class, are we?" Katherine shouts back.

"No, but there are a lot of Romeos and Juliets here."

"Are we all going to die as star-crossed lovers, Mr. Roberts?"

"Don't think so, but I've just broken up a bit of fighting going on between a few 'lovers' on the deck."

"You mean frogs, Mr. Roberts?"

He laughs. "Give me your camera." He snaps Katherine laughing with Liz, Katherine swinging with the beat, Katherine flashing cheesy grins at William. "Have a great night," he winks, handing back the camera.

I will, Mr. Roberts. Katherine looks up at William, who's much taller than her.

Jessie and Greg arrive on the dance floor. Julia comes back, and Liz is still unstoppable with her short guy. William's arms circle Katherine's waist. *I never thought … William. Am I being ridiculous? It's your eyes. And you love the ocean. You've got really special eyes … William.* The name circles inside her head as others return for the last songs, and the floor is filled with movement and dancing.

The lead singer swivels to the guitarist's strings, seducing the microphone with her lips against the wire mesh. William swirls Katherine around and around so that black velvet clings to her as the ferry splashes homeward, sliding through the water.

Rachel and her mother are waiting in the car for Katherine. "How was it?" they ask together.

"The best night. The best."

*The whirlpool pulls her downwards, pulls her. Then there is
a hand. It takes hold of the Beast's hand, dragging her up, but
the hand is gentle, and she moves easily through the whirlpool,
floating upwards with her brown hair softly circling her until she's
in his arms. The Prince holds Katherine.*

Chapter Six

*P*hotomania. Everyone yells, "Show me! Show me!"

"I look so stupid," Julia groans.

"You don't, but Mr. Roberts does." Jessie points, "Just look at him."

"Oh, there's one of you and Greg."

Looking over Jessie's shoulder, Liz interrupts. "William's cute."

Katherine blushes.

"Are you going to go out with him?" asks Liz.

"Don't be an idiot," Katherine mutters.

Photos pass under desks, across aisles, through physics and math and assembly and the last class of the day, English. Mr.

Roberts lifts up his hands, accepting defeat. "All right, I don't think we're going to get very far in class today." He rummages in his briefcase and produces his own photographs. "Now, you Juliets, I think we'll dedicate this lesson to serious study of the dance."

There's so much gossip and laughing that when the bell rings no one's in a hurry to leave, except Katherine. She has an appointment in the city at the doctor's. Packing her bag quickly, she leaves Jessie in charge of the photos and any important information Katherine might miss. "I'll call you later."

When Katherine peers through the glass door into the doctor's waiting room, she sees her mother waiting patiently next to an artificial palm tree. She forces down irritation as she pushes open the glass door, nods at the receptionist who knows her, then makes her way towards the palm tree. She sits next to her mother. "You didn't have to come."

"It was not a problem to leave work early. The manager is very understanding. I will start work early for the shift on Saturday, that is all."

I don't want you to begin earlier. You'll have to get up at five in the morning. Katherine whispers under her breath, "You don't have to anymore." *It makes me feel guilty, and why do you have to anymore?* Katherine rustles through a women's magazine without reading anything. *I'm seventeen, nearly eighteen. I can see the doctor for a checkup without you.*

"Katherine." The receptionist calls out her name. Her mother and Katherine stand up together, and the receptionist smiles. "You look more like your mother every day, Katherine."

"Everyone says that." Katherine glances at her mother, with her olive complexion and dark hair. The Professor acknowledges them as they open the exam room door. He's around sixty, with thinning hair and a softly spoken, slightly nervous tone to his voice. He's also one of the most eminent surgeons in the country.

He commences the examination, interspersed with the usual questions. "How are you?" "Is there any tightening of skin?" "Is biology still your favorite subject?" "Let me check your range of movement." "How's your swimming?" As he raises her right arm, he sees the tear.

Her mother reaches out to touch her daughter. "Katherine, you did not tell me."

Katherine jerks away from her touch. "It's nothing, Mum. And you know I can't have a graft now. Swimming trials are on." Her voice peters out. *I don't want to explain. Don't make me explain.* Katherine presses her hands against her chest. *I feel like I can't breathe. Give me some room, Mum.*

Her mother protests, but stops when the Professor answers, "All right. We can leave it for a little while. You know how to keep it clean."

"I will make sure Katherine looks after herself properly." The Professor nods.

This is humiliating. I don't want the Professor to think I can't look after myself. Mum, I can take care of myself. The Professor writes notes in a thick folder with red tags jutting out in odd places. Katherine watches his old-fashioned fountain pen scratch black on to white paper, then she looks up at her mother. *Mum, you have to let me grow up. You just have to. I can't be your little girl forever.*

It is Tuesday morning, and her mother drops Rachel at school on her way to Mrs. Hampton's. Katherine hasn't started school yet, even though she's six. She loves going with her mother to Mrs. Hampton's, but hates the bus trip there. The bus makes her ill. She's never allowed to eat before she rides on the bus because she feels sick. Her mother tells funny jokes and makes her laugh on the trip so that she doesn't think about throwing up.

Mrs. Hampton lives in a huge house that overlooks Sydney Harbor. Katherine watches the yachts from the balcony. Sometimes Mrs. Hampton is there while her mother cleans. She's always kind to Katherine, wanting to give her ice cream and toys. Katherine accepts the toys, but never the ice cream.

As her mother rubs the window panes, making them sparkle, Mrs. Hampton walks over. She's hesitant. "I hope you won't consider me rude ..." Katherine's mother stops rubbing the panes. "It's just that I've noticed with Katherine ... well ... her hair, her face ... and she's awkward ... can't lift her arm very well ... She can't run properly, can she? Do you ... would you mind taking her to see my doctor?"

Her mother looks at Mrs. Hampton. There's a catch in her voice. "No, I would not mind." She doesn't tell Mrs. Hampton about her many trips to the hospitals. She's gone to so many hospitals in the city, until the doctors won't see her. She doesn't tell her about the pleadings, the arguments, the examinations of Katherine. No one will do anything for her little girl. She overheard them once. "I don't think she understands English. The girl is all right. It's the mother who needs help." They call her pushy, neurotic, but she still takes Katherine back to the hospitals. At the hospitals she speaks in her soft Italian accent to those people standing behind barricades of glass and vinyl. They talk to her slowly, loudly, as if her quiet Italian sounds make her deaf, as if she's ignorant. They tell her, "It's only cosmetic, not covered by the health system … nothing can be done."

"No, I would not mind taking Katherine to your doctor."

Mrs. Hampton calls the doctor's office then. Makes the appointment for that afternoon. "Urgent," she whispers to her family doctor. "Urgent."

Katherine and her mother wait in reception. When the receptionist calls, her mother takes Katherine's hand, and they walk together into the doctor's room. The doctor starts when he sees Katherine. Then he smiles and points to two chairs on the other side of the desk.

Her mother tells him that Katherine can't stand straight anymore, that she sometimes feels sick.

"She shouldn't be ill from the scarring. Are you sick, Katherine?" he asks gently.

She doesn't answer and holds onto her mother's knitted cream jacket.

Her mother takes off her daughter's white top. Katherine's small body bends forward, contorting her stomach so that she holds her stomach when she eats. The doctor examines her, tracing his hand down her head, scarred by ridges and burns. Her neck bends towards her right shoulder as if it is attached to it. She can't straighten fully because scars can't grow or flex like the rest of her.

"I've seen enough."

Katherine's mother presses her hand to her mouth. Slowly she dresses Katherine, then holds her close.

The doctor shakes his head. "A child with this type of scarring. A child who isn't given the chance to grow properly." He mutters under his breath. "We have a health system. The expertise …" Suddenly the doctor is angry. He pulls the phone sharply towards him and calls his friend. A plastic surgeon. "You have to see this little girl now. She can't pay. I'm asking a favor. You owe me. We owe this little girl."

There is so much surgery. Six operations. Her mother is there looking after her, feeding, bathing, telling her stories, running home to Rachel, but coming back early for Katherine so she knows she isn't alone. Her mother leaves her soft knitted jacket with Katherine when she goes to the bathroom or has a break or goes home late in the evening for Rachel, and Katherine cries until she comes back.

Staff at the Burn Unit, doctors, the Professor, do favors and start a series of hair transplants. The doctors graft ten inches of skin onto Katherine's sides, and Katherine can stand straight for the first time in three years. She eats ice cream.

I love you, Mum. You don't know it, but to me, you're a saint.
A real saint, like Joan of Arc. I made it because of you. I am
grateful. More than you can ever know, but I'm older now. I
have to do things myself. Do you understand, Mum? It's taken
a long time, but I am grown up. The Professor examines behind
her knees, her right leg, her stomach, chest. The Professor checks
Katherine's scalp, most of it covered now with her own expanded
skin. She has long hair now. He lifts her hair up to examine her
head with its misshapen scars.

Katherine shuts her eyes tightly, ignores her mother who
is as pale as the painted lilies hanging above her, then she
demands, "I want to wear my hair up." She takes a breath,
opens her eyes. "I want to look like everyone else."

Her mother interrupts as if to protect her, "You do."

You're a liar. "Mum, please don't."

The Professor's black-framed diplomas stare down at
Katherine.

"I don't want to hide scars under my hair. I don't want the
side of my face to be like this. You've helped me before. Please."

"Katherine, I don't know." The Professor scribbles in his
notepad.

"Please. You can help me."

"I don't know about that."

There's tension between Katherine and her mother as they
leave the office. Her mother is angry. "Why did you not tell

me about your arm? You must not swim this year."

"Mum, I don't want to talk about this. If I swim it's my decision, not yours." Katherine slams the car door shut. It's the new family car, which her mother bought after taking them to every car lot in the city. Rachel had said that she was happy. "No more lifts," but she hadn't meant it and still drives Katherine to the beach for practice.

"Please, Katherine. You will hurt our new car. I work hard for this car."

"I work hard too, Mum."

"What is wrong with you? You are upsetting me." Her mother grasps the wheel tightly as she edges out from the curb. The rush hour traffic is heavy with cars beeping and gas fumes seeping into the air.

Katherine shudders. *I can't deal with this.* She turns on the radio. *I don't want to make you angry or upset, Mum, but you make* me *angry and upset. I try to do everything you want. I study, help in the house. I'm starting a job as a waitress on Saturday afternoon. I'll pay for myself now. Let me make my own choices. If I decide to swim, then I'll do it. It's my life, and I'll live with the consequences.* They're on the freeway now, and her mother lessens her grasp on the steering wheel as the traffic flows quickly and smoothly towards the outer suburbs.

"What is this about more surgery, Katherine?"

"I want more done." *I'm not a little girl anymore. I can speak for myself. The way you treated me in front of the*

Professor was embarrassing. How could you? You don't live with scars. I do. I know what it really means; you'll never know. Sometimes I want to hide in a cupboard where it's dark and safe and no one can make me feel ugly. Where I'm invisible. But I don't want to be invisible all my life. I can't live like that. Is that what you want for me, Mum?

She asks Katherine questions. Katherine answers in monosyllables until her mother is annoyed. "This is enough. I am tired from work and rushing to get you to the doctor's, and I have to cook tonight. Is Jessie coming for dinner?"

"Yes."

"Is she staying over tonight?"

"Yes." *Luckily, so I can get away from you.*

Her mother presses her lips closely together and focuses on the road. Katherine looks out of the window, waiting for the familiar stretch of eucalyptus trees and wattle blossoms. They're silent until they reach home.

Rachel is cooking, as usual. "Thought I'd save you the trouble, Mum. Stir-fry chicken in my special sauces. Sound good? By the way, Jessie's here already."

"Thank you, Rachel. There is some watermelon, strawberries and oranges in the fridge. I will make fruit salad. It will cool us all down. Hello, Jessie. How are your parents?"

"Good, thanks."

Jessie and Katherine disappear into Katherine's bedroom. The "Romeo and Juliet" soundtrack hums under the door as Katherine closes it against her mother. She shakes her mother from her mind. *I'm so glad you're here, Jessie. I want to forget about this afternoon.*

Jessie is lounging on the bed. "I like that song, even though it has the dreaded title." She sings with the music.

Katherine swallows hard. *You're not here, Mum. Go away.* Katherine hides behind her closet door and slips on jeans and a T-shirt. "Well, tell me about him."

"About who?" Jessie turns to face Katherine as she sits on the floor next to the bed.

"As if you don't know."

"Do you mean Greg?"

"Who else? Or are you seeing another boy?"

"Never." Jessie dramatically presses her hands against her heart.

Katherine laughs. "You're definitely an actor or drama queen, Jessie. Forget science."

"You know I'd never give up science. Anyway, Greg is picking us up about seven tonight for the play. I can't wait to see him. The more I see him, the cuter he gets. I like his red hair, and I like him." She hugs Katherine's pillow. "It'll be a great night. The play should be good. Better than reading it in class."

"I don't mind reading the play. It gives me time to think. Rereading parts. Getting coffee in the middle of a scene. Thinking about what's happening."

"Mr. Roberts."

"He's a good teacher."

"Sorry, your Romeo is William now, isn't he?"

Katherine grabs the pillow from under Jessie's head, then throws it at her.

She flings it back. Jessie's giggling. "I can't help teasing you."

"It's not funny."

"I think it is." Jessie sits up. "Thanks a lot for letting me stay tonight. I really mean that. Dad would have given me a hard time if he knew I was going to the play with Greg. I'm supposed to concentrate on studies, not him."

"I guess your dad's looking out for you, that's all." *Is Mum looking out for me? Is it OK then?*

"Come on. I have to make my own choices. I want to see Greg. Life isn't just studying, is it? It's not Dad's decision."

Katherine nods. "You're right."

The words from the "Romeo and Juliet" soundtrack make Jessie take a slow breath. "That's so romantic."

Katherine draws a heart in the air. "So how serious are you really, about Greg?" *William hasn't even called me. He probably never will. Why should he?*

"Serious, I guess." Jessie looks around the room. "It's a mess in here, Katherine."

"I've heard that before. Are you going to tell me?"

"I don't know how to explain it, but when Greg's with me I feel special. I love it when he touches me. It makes me shiver. Not a cold shiver. A tingling one." Jessie wraps her arms around herself. "It feels special."

Shiver? Touches? What's that? It's not Mama holding me. It's

71

not Rachel taking my arm. It's not the Professor examining my grafts. Special? Will someone ever want to touch me like that? It'll never happen to me. Katherine runs her hand along the back of her neck. *Someone touching my scars, feeling my arms, my back, the roughness along my neck and under my hair ... seeing me.* Katherine shudders. *I'd be afraid a boy will hate me. William will hate me.*

Jessie lies back on the bed. "I feel safe when Greg holds my hand. That's stupid, but I get a warm feeling inside me."

I can't even imagine someone wanting to be with me. Men? I don't know who they are. I was a baby when my father left. There's just Mum, Rachel, me. No one has even asked me out, and what would I do if someone did? William danced with me. He put his arms around me. Did I feel safe?

"Let's play 'Romeo and Juliet' again."

"I'd like to feel warm, Jessie." Katherine hesitates. "You know, after my burns, my father left."

Jessie nods. "I know."

"Rachel hates him. I don't understand what I feel about him." Katherine touches the roughness along her arms. "After the burns, he came around a few times, and that was it. Never saw him again. How could he just leave? Your father wouldn't leave."

"He'd stay. I guess some men leave when there are problems."

"He sends us birthday cards." *I don't want to talk about him. Why am I?* "Rachel's got his red hair and freckles. I'm glad I look like Mum. He's never helped us. Rachel remembers him." Katherine stops abruptly.

72

"You don't need him, Katherine."

"Maybe you're right."

Katherine's relieved when Rachel calls them for dinner. The chicken is spicy, a mix of basil and chili. Everyone drinks jugs of water. The fruit salad is cool, and the sweet pink of the watermelon takes the bite out of the red chili.

"Sorry, Mum, about being in a bad mood before." *I love you. Where would I be without you?* Katherine gets up from the table and starts clearing the dishes.

The doorbell rings. Greg. There are awkward "hellos" and the usual greeting talk.

"Don't worry about the dishes." "Are you looking forward to seeing the play?" "When will you be home?" "Have a good time." "Drive carefully." "What time will you be home again?" They escape through the front door.

Chapter Seven

$\mathcal{K}$atherine speaks to the coach about swimming at regionals one day and maybe even nationals. He wants to talk to her about it after the trials. "I'll see how well you do and how serious you are."

Swimming practice is five mornings a week before school. Then there is the gym and push-ups and strengthening exercises. After studying, Katherine runs in the evenings, when it's cooler. She always runs the same route, down along the ghost gum track, startling rabbits when she whistles to the gray and pink galahs perched on high branches.

Sometimes Katherine has to miss practice. Sometimes she doesn't go to the gym, but she always runs. "You won't be a winner if you're not totally committed," the coach shouts. He concentrates on other swimmers who never miss practice. They miss school instead. They don't have a weekend job, doctor appointments, shopping trips into the city, hospitalizations.

She doesn't argue with the coach, but he shakes her purpose. *Committed? Am I?* Katherine's tear doesn't heal, even though she's careful to treat it properly. She won't let her mother see it, and they fight until her mother shouts at her, and Katherine slams her bedroom door.

On Saturday she argues with Rachel over the mess Katherine has left in the bathroom, studies two hours of math, goes to the gym, calls Jessie, who seems to have endless things to say about Greg. "He's the most interesting boy in the world," Katherine jokes. Then it's Saturday afternoon. The cafe. Escape from her mother's pressure. Financial independence.

Katherine has to wear black trousers and a long-sleeved white shirt. She likes the uniform, which gives her protection from the curiosity of people who pretend not to look at the scarring of her arms and legs. The manager doesn't mind that she wears her hair down.

The cafe isn't too busy. Two ladies sit eating vegetarian sandwiches on whole wheat bread. A man in the corner reads his newspaper and sips a cappuccino. There are three tables outside, with four director's chairs under each of them. Katherine goes to the back of the cafe, says hello to the cook, then puts on a black apron and starts wiping down counters in tune with the music playing on the radio. She's staring out of the window when a crowd of people sit down at the outside tables. She has already discovered that's the way it is in a cafe. Flood or famine. Katherine gets the menus, and as she hands them out she sees him. Marc.

"Didn't know you worked here," Marc says casually.

Don't blush, Katherine, don't you dare, but she feels her face getting hot. "Started last week. This is my second Saturday."

They order burgers, colas, make jokes. "We're going to the beach. I do surfboat rowing for the lifesavers," he stammers. "I hear you're a good swimmer. You'd like surf sports."

Are you trying to be nice? Is that you, Marc? "I can swim."

Katherine doesn't wait for a response, escaping into the cafe, only coming out to clear dishes. When she leaves the check on the table, Marc looks at her as if he wants to say something. He doesn't. There is a tip for Katherine. She watches them disappear around the corner. *That was awful, Marc.* She blocks him out as she wipes down his table. *Don't come back.*

It is the regional clubs' swimming meet. Jessie's going to be there for the big event. Rachel insists on driving her beaten-up car, not her mother's new Ford. "My car deserves to be there after all those times she's driven Katherine to practice."

"Is it a person?" Katherine laughs.

"Well, nearly."

The southerly wind whips up the surf, which pounds against the beach sand. The sea water of the pool ripples as if in anticipation. There are crowds, coaches, swimmers, local newspapers, excitement. The microphone blares for competitors to get ready. Freestyle, backstroke, breast stroke, butterfly, relays, medleys. 100 meters, 200 meters, 400 meters, 800 meters. Heats. Heats. Semi finals.

Finals. Eight swimmers. Katherine's rubber cap adheres like glue. Synthetic nylon molds onto her body, so there's no definition between body, swimsuit, swimsuit, body. No friction; fast. Eight pairs of legs on starting blocks. Katherine looks out to the sea, then bends forward. Waiting. Waiting. Katherine sees only blue expanding into the horizon. She does not see her mother in the stands, her sister's banner, Jessie waving, the coach's raised fists. There is only Katherine, the water, the horizon … the starting gun.

The coach roars from the side of the pool as Katherine sucks in air hard, blowing out air hard. Her arms strain, edging against seconds that tick like a bomb in her head. Tick. Tick. Faster. Extra effort. More effort. More.

One. Two. They pass her. *I have to get there first. Faster, Katherine, faster. Catch up.* Her teammate is number three. Four passes her. The swimmers' wake forces water against her face until she can't see the horizon. Too many swimmers in front. Slower. Her arms ache. Crowds shout for the winners - first, second, third place. Splashing. Number five touches the wall. Katherine is number six. She pulls off her cap, dives under the water, re-emerging with her hair smooth against her head.

She nods at the coach and other teammates and her mother, but she can't hear them, see them. She climbs the rough iron ladder out of the pool, heading for the athletes' area. The locker room is splintered with talking and changing and preparing for other races. She locks herself into a shower cubicle. Turns on the water. Quiet. *Sixth.* Only the running of water down her face, her back, splashing against white tiles, swirling down the corroded iron drain. *Sixth. Is this it?*

"To reach the final is terrific," Jessie congratulates her.

Katherine listens as her mother and Jessie talk at her about the race and swimming. Rachel looks at her sister. "It's OK, Katherine."

Rachel changes the conversation. "Does anyone want some gum?"

Jessie takes a piece.

Katherine shakes her head. "No." She turns away. "Thanks."

The final race is swum. The coach meets his swimmers for a postmortem, with congratulations for some, a rallying of spirits for others, offers for others, more practice for everyone. As Katherine wraps her towel around her and turns to walk off with some of her teammates, the coach calls her over. "I know how you can lose extra seconds off your time, Katherine."

As always, she hides inside the protection of her towel. She presses an edge of the towel under her arm. Surprising herself, she answers, "I'm not fast enough." *That's the truth. The truth.* Katherine looks away from the coach. A surfboat smashes against the waves, oars paddling furiously, being thrown up, half-jutting into space, crashing into troughs, lurching, spiraling, winning against the sea.

"Just surfers. Would you listen, Katherine?" The coach shakes his head. "If you want it enough, you can be faster."

"I came sixth." *Do I feel all right about that? Maybe. I made the finals. That's an achievement. I'm just not as fast, as committed as the others. Can I accept that?*

"You're fast."

"Not fast enough." *What's this about? I've never been your star swimmer anyway.*

"You'd have to train harder than you are doing now. It's tough, but you could swim for the nationals, maybe even Australia."

Katherine shakes her head.

"I'd like you to apply for entry into …" the coach hesitates a little, "the Paralympic Games."

She looks confused, remembering wheelchairs and crutches. After practice sessions, she'd say hello to these athletes in the locker room, and they'd say hello back to her.

"If you get in, you'd win the 100-meter and 200-meter freestyle and maybe others."

Katherine observes the black stopwatch the coach holds in his rough hands. Too much sun has freckled his arms, blotching blondish hair and brown spots right up to his elbows. *I don't like your hands, Coach.* Her eyes dart to his face, to the watch, back to his face. *I don't like you.*

"Australia's the leading country for those games. You'll win gold. I know it."

Gold? Winning? Is that what winning is? I don't like you, Coach. She runs her fingers under her hair, touching the side of her face. "But those athletes are in wheelchairs or blind or …" *Am I the same? Am I?*

"I'd organize things. I think you could qualify."

"Qualify?" She runs her fingers over the scars on her thigh. *Is that what you see when I'm on the starting block? When my arms are stretching through the water, is that what you see? Scars?* Suddenly panic grips her stomach, and she bends forward. *Mama, help me. I'm scared.* She repeats, confused, "Qualify?" *Rachel, there's a man here calling me Mud Face, Frankenstein, Pineapple. Am I so different?*

"I want you to seriously think about it."

The night is warm, but Katherine shivers. She looks up at the coach. *I don't like you, Coach. I don't like you.* "It'd be cheating." *I think I hate you, Coach.*

The school is a brown two-story building with steps disappearing into corridors and closed doors. Children fly down the steps like bees on a mission from their hive. They stop to stare at Katherine, who holds onto her mother's skirt. They flap and flutter before they continue their flight onto the green playground or the lunch line.

Her mother is wearing her cream jacket, knitted by Nonna.

Katherine loves that jacket, and when terrible monsters frighten her in the night, her mother gives it to her. In the morning the jacket is crushed and warm. Her mother irons it then.

They have an appointment with the principal. The secretary tells them to wait. Katherine wanders around the room, investigating timetables pinned on a board and a lime green playing block that is stuck under a bookcase.

The secretary tells Katherine's mother that they can go into the office. The principal stands when they enter. Motioning to two brown vinyl chairs, he stiffly introduces himself before sitting down in his swivel chair. He bends forward, resting his hands on the brown wooden desk. Protected by a computer, a stack of multicolored files, a phone and the paraphernalia of his job, he starts, "I have discussed Katherine with the Education Department." He presses his hands together. "She's an unusual case. We haven't the backup staff to really cater for her special needs."

"What do you mean?" Her mother takes Katherine's hand.

"Well, she's got … How can I explain? You understand."

"No, I do not understand." She strokes Katherine's head, and Katherine smiles.

"She's not quite … Her movement is restricted. She can't play like the other children, can she?"

"That is untrue."

"There needs to be a special education teacher allocated to help her with her work." He fidgets. "With her writing, at least."

"Katherine can write her name already, and a lot of other

*things. In two languages, she can write." She turns to her
daughter. "Come here, Katherine. Show the man that you can
write in English and Italian."*

*"No, please don't. I'm sorry, but this is really getting us
nowhere." He clears his throat. "We have no facilities for disabled
children."*

*Her mother leaves confused, holding Katherine's hand tightly.
She walks past the secretary without acknowledging her, through
the corridors, down the steps, past the children flying back into
their hive, over the grassy playing fields to the yellow-posted bus
stop.*

"Am I going to Rachel's school, Mama?"

"We will see."

*There are phone calls and meetings and letters. Community
Services says, "No, your daughter isn't disabled. No, she doesn't
qualify for any assistance. No, there is no disability allowance.
Yes, you should enroll her in a local school."*

*The Education Department says, "No, your daughter is
disabled. She can't go to a local school unless a principal agrees."*

*Katherine says, "You read to me, Mama." "Rachel, you play
ball with me." "I don't like them. They're staring at me." "Am I
going to school?"*

The principals say, "No."

*But then there is one principal who hesitates, listens. She says
she'd like to meet Katherine.*

*With both Rachel and Katherine beside her, their mother
stands outside the principal's office. "Come in." The principal*

catches her breath for a moment when she sees Katherine with her head exposed, unprotected by hair. "How nice to have you girls visit." She hands Rachel and Katherine a picture book. Rachel, who is ten, sits on a mat in the corner and reads to her sister the story of how the kangaroo found his tail. Katherine points to the drawings in the book, raising her hand. But she can only reach halfway. She giggles with her sister at the pictures of cheeky possums and wise old owls. The principal watches the girls for a while. Then she turns to ask their mother about Katherine.

"Yes, Katherine does fall over sometimes. Yes, it is hard for Katherine to stretch her arm fully, to run as fast as the others. Yes, Katherine becomes upset sometimes, but Katherine tries everything. She is a happy girl. Katherine is happy, even though she has been through so much. Katherine wants to learn, to go to school. You will like Katherine. You will like her. You will. You will."

"I'm sure I will." The principal asks the secretary to bring them coffee. The girls don't notice that their mother is quietly crying, and that the principal has her arm around her.

Rachel leaves her old school. She's sad to say goodbye to her friends, but there'll be other friends at the new school, and there is Katherine to look after.

The three of them wait at the bus stop. Katherine and Rachel are wearing the new school uniforms their mother bought them from the secondhand shop. Katherine loves the neatly ironed blue-checkered dress that smells of soap and lavender, but Rachel isn't so sure. She misses her old gray skirt and white blouse.

Katherine is holding her mother's hand tightly when they see the bus come around the corner. Their mother bends to kiss Rachel, then Katherine. "You girls be good at the new school," she says, as she gently pushes Katherine towards the bus.

Rachel takes her sister's hand. "We're always good, Mama."

"I know you are." Their mother's voice quivers.

She waves as her girls climb the bus steps together. They wave back from their seat. Katherine presses her nose against the pane, making it flat.

"I love you," she whispers.

Chapter Eight

"Nonna and Grandpapa are coming out to Australia for Christmas." *I know, Mum. You've told us ten times already. They are only coming at the end of the year.* "It will be different to their Italian Christmas, but we will have good food and be together. I have to arrange holidays from my job because everyone wants the holidays then. The garden will need some work. Nonna is a great gardener. Katherine, you will have to move in with Rachel."

Rachel says under her breath as she stacks the dishes, "I like my room." She knows Katherine will take over. No one hears her.

As her mother wipes down the kitchen counters, she

reminisces about eating crusty panini on the rocky seawall with her grown-up brother, visiting the big city of Genoa with its parks and palaces, playing with her cousins among the fishing nets. "Grandpapa loves the sea and the turquoise water and fishing boats. He will love the harbor of Sydney too." She laughs like a girl. "Your nonna was so angry when Grandpapa would disappear. Where do you think he went, Katherine?" She doesn't wait for her answer. "To his favorite place, looking from the cliffs far out to sea." She catches her breath. "He would take me with him sometimes."

"You miss it, don't you?"

She brushes back her hair lightly. "Yes, Katherine, but Australia is home. I could not go back." Every week, for as long as the girls can remember, there has been a phone call from Italy. Now that her mother is working full time, she phones them as well.

Imagine leaving home at nineteen, all by yourself, for a man on the other side of the world. A man you really didn't know, who visited with his backpack and a promise of freedom.

Their mother is always telling them that there is no hurry to marry, that they have to have careers and be a person first. "I married your father against my parents' wishes. Grandpapa was strict. He loved his church and the family meals and wanted me to marry one day a boy from our way of life."

"But you ran away with our father."

"Yes, and I broke my parents' hearts."

"And he left you and us."

"Yes."

"Was it worth it?"

She strokes her younger daughter's face gently. "You and Rachel are worth it."

"Look, we've company, Mum." Katherine goes to the back door to watch the red-blue rosellas pecking at seeds on the grass. With their bright colors and cheeky parrot beaks, they always seem like they're partying.

"I must go to the garden. There are weeds." As their mother starts to walk to the shed for her gardening tools, she turns to Katherine. "Have you made an appointment with the Professor to look at your arm yet?"

Don't ruin things. Don't. Katherine looks at her hands, trying to control this rising anger. She doesn't want to be angry but … *I can't stand you always checking, arranging things for me. I love you, but stop controlling me.* "I'm seeing the Professor next week."

"Make sure you tell me when the appointment is."

Her mother takes her spade and goes into the backyard. The rosellas flap a little as she disturbs them, then they return to their pecking.

Katherine shakes her head. She switches on the kettle, gets two mugs, heaps a teaspoon of coffee into each, takes milk from the fridge, and waits for the kettle to boil. Calming down, she watches her mother bend over the garden beds, turning the bush soil that's been fertilized so that soft-petaled roses can grow. A golden butterfly flits past her.

"Coffee," Katherine announces, as she enters Rachel's room. Music plays quietly in her sister's room. Teeth are neatly lined on a shelf. Stacked next to them are magazines. There's a photo of the three of them and one of her grandparents. A photo with her friend Jill. No boyfriend. A vase of jasmine splashes perfume through the room. Rachel is sitting at her desk studying for her exams. Katherine hands her a mug. "It's got marshmallows in it."

"Thanks. I'm glad the weather's not so hot anymore. I can stand hot coffee again." She spoons out a sticky marshmallow from her cup. "You were really good at the swimming meet."

"Sure." They both understand the half-lie, half-truth.

A wispy breeze makes the pale blue curtains flutter. "Mum's happy about our grandparents coming. It'll be strange having them here, especially Grandpapa."

Rachel talks about that Christmas they spent in Italy, until Katherine interrupts.

"I want to ask you something." Katherine places her mug carefully onto a small table, then sits on the floor. There are no books or clothes scattered everywhere, like in her room. She runs one hand over the soft aqua carpet. "I've been … reconsidering … swimming. It was good to get into the finals. You've been so good to me … driving me … early mornings … training … at the meets. It's meant a lot to me, even though I don't tell you." She waits. "I thought about this all last night. Didn't sleep much. But I know something now. I'm as fast as I'll ever be." Katherine presses her hands into the carpet so that pile sticks through her fingers. "It's my scars … I'm fighting against my own skin."

Silently, they look at each other.

"The coach said something that's forced me to face who I am … what I want to be … if I can be anything …" The words come disjointedly, like when she was very little, before the climbing bar fall.

"What is it?" Rachel puts her mug down on her desk.

Breathing deeply, Katherine speaks quietly, as if still working out her thoughts. "The coach said I'd win. That I should swim with the Paralympics. Am I that? Is that me?" She raises her right arm. The early years of wearing the elastic burn suit over her small body, the creams, the grafts, haven't taken away scars of third degree.

"You got to the finals. I could never do that."

"I don't want to swim any more competitions. It's not that I'm disappointed. Well, I am. I've worked hard for it, but the coach forced me to look at myself. I'm different from the rest of the squad."

"Katherine, you're more than them."

"I just can't swim for the team anymore."

They listen to the music for a while. Katherine gets up and pretends to flick through the magazines on her sister's shelf. "Maybe I'll do something with the surf. Lifesaving? They're always looking for new members, and I'd feel good to do something worthwhile, not just for myself."

Rachel nods. "They'll want you."

"I don't know."

"Come on, Katherine. You've already proved you're a champion. Forget about the coach."

Champion? Forget? Katherine flashes Rachel an angry look. "Easy for you to forget."

"That's unfair." Rachel doesn't forget anything.

Katherine presses her hands against the shelf. "Sorry. I'm just feeling … I've worked so hard. But you're right. Who cares about the coach?"

"No one."

"No one." Katherine repeats Rachel's words uncertainly.

They're silent. Rachel slips into her role naturally, supporting Katherine. She gets up and stands beside her sister. "It'll be something new. You've always loved the ocean." She nudges Katherine. "More importantly, who's driving you to lifesaving practice?"

Katherine half-smiles. "You're driving me, of course. But it won't be at five in the morning anymore."

"Do you mean earlier?"

Katherine laughs, and everything feels all right in Rachel's room.

Katherine makes more coffee with marshmallows. "Maybe I should get the graft done under my arm now. Stop Mum pressuring me all the time."

"You have to anyway."

Katherine touches the right side of her face. "When I see the Professor I'm going to ask him about this." She lifts up her hair, exposing scars. The skin is tight, pulling at her face, shoulder and neck, rippling under her hair. "Do you think he can do something?"

"I don't know. Maybe. I'm sure if he can, he will." Rachel stares at her exam notes, then picks up the coffee mugs to take them to the kitchen.

Katherine goes to the bathroom, and when she comes back she's laughing. "Do you remember this, Rachel?"

"How can anyone forget that?"

"I found it at the back of the bathroom cabinet. Haven't seen it for years."

"It looks dead." Rachel shakes her head as Katherine flashes the small hairpiece in the air.

"The glue isn't great anymore. Look, Rachel." She sticks it onto her arm. "Hairy days ahead."

"That's a hopeless joke."

Katherine strokes the hairy scalp. "What about making some more braid? You could braid my arm."

"You're making me laugh. I'll drop my coffee."

"Do you remember that afternoon in the city, when it fell off my head?"

"Katherine, I could hardly forget it. Jessie couldn't stop laughing, especially when she asked that old man if he'd seen a scalp lying around the street. He thought she was an axe murderer who sliced off parts of people's bodies. Everyone was looking for that stupid thing. You were bad when you asked that policeman for help."

"Well, it cost Mum a lot of money to get it made. Just feel that rubber and look at the color of the hair. Very natural. It's a top-of-the-line scalp. Except it kept falling off. It looks good on my arm, don't you think?"

"If you're a gorilla."

Katherine pretends to eat a banana, making Rachel laugh. "Where did we find it after all that, Katherine?"

"It was the policeman. Remember? The scalp was in the gutter." Katherine speaks to her arm. "Come on, hairy arm. Let's change the song to 'Romeo and Juliet.' We'll be at the cutting edge of music."

"Cutting? Your jokes are getting worse."

Katherine detaches the scalp from her arm and puts it down.

"Come on, let me get on with my work." Rachel goes back to her dental notes.

"I've got to study too." Katherine slumps onto the carpet next to her sister. She opens her Shakespeare, "'Love give me strength! and strength shall help afford.'" Katherine looks across at Rachel. "What do you believe love is?"

"Us, Katherine."

They smile at each other.

When the phone rings, Katherine's engrossed with the passions of Romeo and Juliet's undying love.

"Do you want to get it?" Rachel's annoyed.

There's no answer.

"Are you deaf or something?" Rachel leaves her notes and picks up the phone. "Katherine. It's for you. William."

Katherine throws down her book.

"Oh, I see you're not deaf." Rachel puts her hand over the mouth piece. "Who's William?"

Katherine jumps up. "Tell you later." Running into her bedroom, she closes the door, shoves books aside, sits on the floor with her back against the wall. *OK, it's probably nothing. He just wants to catch up. I saw him at the bus stop the other day. He probably saw me too.* "Hi, William."

"Hi, Katherine. I had a good time at the dance. Did you?"

"Yes." *Why didn't you call before? I've been waiting. I thought you didn't like me.*

"I was meaning to call, but I had assignments to finish, and I had the basketball competition. We got to the semi-finals."

"I'm starting surf-lifesaving."

"Sounds great."

The conversation jerks awkwardly between surfing, hockey and basketball, gradually flowing into school subjects, teachers, friends in common, the latest films. *Are we going to talk forever? Are you going to ask me out? Please ask me out.* "Well, I've got to go, William."

"Me too." There's a pause. "Do you want to go to the movies?" There's another pause. "Maybe with a few friends?"

He's asked me. He's asked me. "Sure. I can talk to Jessie and

Greg." *Get a date. A time.* "When?"

"Is Saturday night OK? Say I pick you up about seven?"

No. No. Think quick. I don't want Mum to give me a lecture about going out. "Can I meet you at the cafe where I work? On High Street. I finish at six."

"So, see you Saturday then."

Slamming done the phone, Katherine runs into her sister's room. "Rachel, Rachel, Rachel. Guess what? Guess? William asked me out, on Saturday. My first Saturday night date." Then it's all out. "He's tall, short brown hair. He plays sports, and he's got really straight white teeth, except he's got a yellow front tooth. That doesn't matter. It makes him interesting, a surfer, he's in his last year, do you think he likes me?"

Chapter Nine

*I*t's the last lesson on "Romeo and Juliet." Mr. Roberts asks the class, "Did you enjoy the theater production?"

Julia calls out, "Loved the play. It was better than reading it. It was so sad."

"'Good night, good night! Parting is such sweet sorrow / That I shall say good night till it be morrow.' Love isn't so easy, is it? Why?" Mr. Roberts points to Jessie.

"Their parents ruined it for Romeo and Juliet. Their families hated each other. It just couldn't work."

"You're right, Jessie." Mr. Roberts recites the last lines of the play. "'For never was a story of more woe / Than this of Juliet and her Romeo.' They both died in the end."

"Fate doomed them. I don't believe in that," Liz calls out.

"Can you control everything? Are some things predetermined?" Mr. Roberts strides up the aisle.

Katherine raises her hand. "Some things you can't change, like who you're born to. Romeo and Juliet came from rich and powerful families. That was good fate. Their families hated each other, and that was bad fate." Katherine hesitates. "They did the rest themselves."

"So you think it's their fault that they died?" Julia rolls her eyes. "Can't believe you think that."

"They didn't have to die. They had a choice." Katherine unconsciously presses her hand against the rough of her neck. *Choice. You don't understand, Julia. You haven't been there. How could you know anything? I've got burns that go so deep, I can't feel my body in places. I've got scars. Scars that make people move away from me, or feel sorry for me, or ... I don't know, treat me differently. I have to choose all the time, every day ... Choose to be like my body ... tight, choking, tearing when I reach out ...* Katherine digs her fingernails into the desk. *I have to choose to stay burned or not. But I'm not burned inside. I'm perfect inside. Can't you see I'm perfect inside?*

Katherine turns away from the classroom and looks out of the window. There is a huge fig tree spreading shade across the pavement in the courtyard. *I don't like pavement. I want to kick it sometimes. I just want to kick things. The pit, my father, Jessie's pretty hair, Rachel, even Mum. I don't like being burned. Fate? I didn't ask for this. I don't want my scars.* Katherine pinches the roughness of her thigh until Mr. Roberts disturbs her thoughts. He's calling out to the class to pay attention. There is an essay he is assigning. Katherine forces herself to look away from the pavement, along the thick, knotty roots of the fig tree, up the rugged trunk sprouting branches and green leaves. She grits her teeth. *You're breaking up the pavement, aren't you, fig tree? You're a big, old fighter. Me too. Guess what, fig tree? I'm not going to be stuck with third degree forever.*

"The essay topic is: Do the lovers control their destiny?"
Yes, Mr. Roberts. Yes. Yes.

"'Love and Destiny' is a great topic to begin with."
"Love and Life" is even better.

Mr. Roberts winks as he collects his books. "I saw a few starstruck lovers at the last dance."

"I wish it was me," Katherine says under her breath.

"Greg and I won't have the same end as Romeo and Juliet," Jessie giggles.

Katherine is quiet as they walk out of the classroom. *Love and life. No, Love of life. That's what I'm choosing.* She asks Jessie, "Can you and Greg come to the movies on Saturday?"

"To see what?"

"Doesn't matter. Anything." She bends her head. "William is taking me."

Jessie gives a muffled scream, making Katherine smile. *Love of life.*

"Fantastic. Terrific. So tell me everything, Katherine. Everything."

"Marc came into the cafe. I'll tell you about that later, but about William …"

"I'll do the graft for your arm in two weeks." The Professor writes his notes. He phones through to his secretary to arrange for the hospital admission, then he gives his attention to Katherine and her mother. He speaks carefully. "Your hair from the extended skin transplants covers the scarring on your neck and head and the right side of your face. There has been a lot of work already done. Further reconstruction is difficult and only succeeds to a point. It may not be successful."

Katherine studies the framed charts hanging on the office walls: color diagrams of facial and limb reconstructions, circulatory responses in burn patients, variations of epidermis thickness. Then she looks at the Professor. *You can do it.*

"However, there is a procedure that I've been developing." The Professor's white eyebrows edge together. "It's painful and may not produce the results you want. Do you realize that?"

Katherine nods. *You can do it. I just know it.* Her mother presses her daughter's hand.

Methodically, the Professor explains. "I would have to graft new skin and tissue onto your shoulder, neck and face in separate operations. You already understand grafting and that it fails sometimes. The blood supply may not develop sufficiently to sustain the grafts. Even if it is successful, grafts often may not look like what you want. There would have to be further surgery, especially to define and reshape." He opens the palms of his hands in a gesture of concern. "I want you both to think about it, talk about it. I'm prepared to go ahead, but only if you understand that it may be a disappointment. For now, let's wait until after this graft, then we can discuss it further."

They leave. Katherine races to catch the elevator in the corridor. She holds open the heavy metal doors for her mother. The doors close. It's stuffy inside the elevator, which is going up before it goes down. Shiny stainless steel and paneled mirrors reflect an anxious fortyish woman with her dark hair in a loose bun, wearing a skirt and cream jacket, and a young woman in jeans and a black T-shirt with her hair hanging loosely around her face.

"Mum, I have to have more surgery done. I want it." She puts the palm of her hand against her face.

"The Professor has always been kind. He never treated me differently because I spoke with an accent. He always explains what is to happen." Looking at her daughter, she says quietly, "It will be painful, Katherine. You may be disappointed." She rubs her forehead with an embroidered handkerchief. "It is hot in here."

It's hot inside. The room is unbearable. Temperatures are raised because Katherine's cold, so cold.

Scrub suits, caps, masks, plastic aprons, people in the room smelling of iodine and soap. Gloved hands immerse Katherine in the hydrotherapy tank. Strangers' hands and Mama's hands.

Katherine whimpers as the warm water is sponged over her wounds. The narcotics dull her movements as she tries to reach for her mother.

"Katherine, you are such a good baby. You are so good and pretty. You have to be really brave because it will be over soon. Over soon." Her mother starts to sing softly to her, but she stops when she sees the nurse coming with her scissors and forceps. Humming, she strokes Katherine's hand.

Blisters opened. Dying tissue stripped away. The smell of decay. Bleeding. Stinging cream. Katherine screaming. Screaming as only a baby can scream. Her mother hovering over her child, sobbing with her baby's sobs.

The elevator opens. The modern glass foyer is busy with people moving between consulting rooms, pathology collections, administration.

"It'll work. Please, Mum."

Her mother sighs as she steps onto the walkway. Plain, black, useful pavement. She turns her back on the glass house of busyness and looks at her daughter. "Yes, if that is what you really want."

"I do, Mum. I do."

Saturday afternoon. Rachel has made a black and silver hair ribbon for Katherine.

"What are you wearing for the big date?"

"Just my black work pants and my favorite green top." Katherine grabs her small stuffed sheepdog. "Hey, what do you think, Pup? Will my green top bring me luck? What do you think?"

Rachel pats Pup's head. "Pup says you don't need luck. Hold still, so I can put this through your hair." She carefully loops it into a knot. "Have you told Mum?"

"Sort of. She knows I'm going to the movies with Jessie and some other friends. I'm not telling her about William yet. I might hate him, so why go through all the boring lectures like 'Be careful with boys,' 'Study is more important than men,' 'You'll have plenty of time afterwards.' Rachel, I'm seventeen and never been kissed. Except for Pup." She looks seriously into Pup's brown marble eyes. "And I made the first move, didn't I, Pup? I don't want you to be the only man in my life. Can you cope with that?"

Rachel's quiet because she's been kissed. But it didn't work out. She had to be there for her mother and sister. She looks at Katherine and smiles. "I've finished your hair. Looks great. Come on then, I'm driving you to the cafe today. I've got a dental association meeting tonight, so I'll be in the car anyway."

Katherine throws Pup onto her bed. "Don't worry, Pup, I'll tell you all about what happens tonight. Hope you don't mind, but we'll just be friends from now on. Is that all right?" She puts her top in her bag. "Let's go."

Their mother is preparing some dips. Two of her girlfriends are coming over.

"We're leaving now, Mum."

"Please be home by midnight, both of you. I will wait up."

"I'll be back by nine." Rachel rattles her keys.

"You don't have to stay up for me." Katherine's voice is edgy.

"Let's go." Rachel grabs her sister's arm.

They drive along the familiar streets of suburbia, streets like the one they live in. Comfortable roads and avenues with lawns being mowed, cars washed, gardens tended, bikes ridden down sidewalks. Birds of paradise flaunt their orange petals and blue stamens, challenging the complacency of ordered flower beds. Speed bumps and roundabouts with *One Way* signs, double yellow lines, roadworks – things are changing. Katherine smiles to herself. *William.*

They reach the strip of traditional shops: the greengrocer's with its array of apples, oranges, melons; the butcher's display of lamb, beef, sausages; the florist overflowing with pink carnations, red roses, violets, golden daffodils. Cafe Smooth's austere modernism: Its black and white colors and minimalist settings contrast with the old-fashioned shops. Rachel drops her sister at the cafe.

The afternoon seems long, and Katherine keeps looking at the beige-faced clock. She serves an old lady Earl Gray tea. It gets busy then. After she gives the girl with a nose ring a banana smoothie, she notices it's already five o'clock. She starts cleaning up. At five thirty, she locks the doors. Her pay is left in the register in an envelope. A shiver runs down her back as she opens the register and puts the bills in her purse. Independence.

The cook's clashing of pots and plates echoes across the tiled cafe floor. Katherine gets ready for her first date – the green top, makeup, perfume. *I'm nervous. I never thought anyone would ever ask me out. Does my hair cover my face? Do I look all right? I don't. I wish Rachel was here. She'd tell me if I look all right. Mum always says I'm beautiful, which is useless.* Katherine talks to the art deco mirror that hangs behind the cappuccino machine. *Why is William taking me out anyway? He's so good-looking, he could ask anyone. I bet he won't turn up. No, that's stupid. He'll turn up because Greg's his friend. He doesn't like me. He didn't mean to ask me out. How could he be so cruel? I'm not going. When Jessie comes, I'll say I've got a cold. She'll just have to go without me.*

There's a knock on the cafe's closed door. Jessie's forehead is pressed against the glass. *You're early. It's only five forty-five.* Katherine unlocks the door. Greg's standing behind Jessie, and William's behind him. *Panic.*

"Are you ready, Katherine?"

"Yes." Katherine calls out to the cook that she's going.

"Right," echoes from the kitchen.

William stands awkwardly next to Greg. His hands are in his pockets. *Am I supposed to go up to him? What am I supposed to do?* Jessie threads her arm through Katherine's. "What movie do you want to see?"

That is Greg's cue to say he wants to see "Batman" and Jessie's to argue that she'd like to see a "meaningful" film. "Batman's meaningful. He always gets the bad guys."

"Sure." Jessie's laughing. She unthreads her arm from Katherine's as she gets into Greg's car. William and Katherine sit in the back seat. *Lucky for movies. They talk about films.* Katherine relaxes a little, and William takes his hands out of his pockets. She glances at his eyes to check. *Hazel. I love hazel eyes.*

They end up seeing "Batman." Katherine screams in the frightening parts, and William takes her hand. Then he doesn't let it go. *Your hand is so big, sort of rough. Is that what men's hands are like?* She glances at him as the Batmobile races through Gotham City. *My stomach is butterflies. William. I really love your name and your hands.*

"You owe me coffee and cake after forcing me to see that, Greg," Jessie complains, as they walk down the red-carpeted stairs out of the theater.

"Come on, you have to admit the special effects were fantastic. Virtual reality is …"

"I know, fantastic." Jessie puts her arm through Greg's. "You're my crazy computer fanatic."

The cinema complex oozes people into the street, everyone shoving as groups move one way or another. William takes Katherine's hand again. "Don't want you to get lost." They follow Jessie and Greg until the crowds ease, and they can wander slowly past the shops which are still open at eleven – bookshops, music shops, cafes, game arcades with machines blaring colors and action. The scent of coffee draws them to a window layered with glass shelves. White meringues are piled high into a pyramid. Smooth dark chocolate covers the Sacher torte. Cherries and rich cream seep from the chocolate Bavarian. Thick lemon frosting layers the orange and poppy seed cake.

"Lemon meringue pie for me," Jessie announces.

"Greedy."

They sit at a table inside. "I'll share if you're all nice to me."

They eat lemon meringue pie and chocolate cake and drink frothy cappuccino while dissecting the technology involved in creating "Batman" and virtual reality. Greg and Jessie get caught up in talking about the latest computers.

"Do you want some more chocolate cake?" William asks.

Katherine shakes her head. "Are you studying a lot now?"

"I'm supposed to be, but I keep thinking about after the exams, when I'm going north. I spend too much time at the beach."

"I like the beach. I'm thinking of doing something in the surf. Maybe, lifesaving." But Katherine doesn't want to talk about herself, or the little she knows about lifesaving. She pushes William's conversation into surfing stories of waxed boards in big swells, riding too close to rocks and cliff faces, searching for the special wave, the left-hand tubes on a reef break. His hazel eyes glint with green and brown flashes as he talks about it. But it isn't bragging. It's something else, something to do with chasing the surf, catching that wave.

Katherine hardly understands his freedom, but she senses the liberation of streets without sidewalks, lawns that are just bush, wild gardens of native flowers. *I want yellow wattle. Kookaburras. Golden butterflies.*

"The guys and I just stick our gear in a car, usually mine, and we go."

You're lucky. No mother telling you what to do. No hospitals. Just your mates. Katherine looks at her watch. Eleven-thirty. "I have to be home by midnight." She reaches into her bag to pay. "I've got money now that I work," she announces.

"Well, keep it. We're paying." William stands.

"That doesn't seem fair."

"Next time, you girls can pay. That's right, isn't it, Greg?"

"Next time."

Greg and Jessie wait in the car as William walks Katherine to the door. She doesn't put the key into the lock because she knows her mother will be in the family room waiting for her, listening for the key. "I had a good time, William."

"Me too." He brushes her hair away from her face making her instinctively shudder. He bends his head towards her. She pulls her hair back over her face wanting to hide when his lips touch hers. *Sweet. You taste so sweet. Chocolate and coffee.* She doesn't resist. The kiss feels warm and tender.

She puts the key in the lock. Turns around to watch him walk to the car, then turns away and goes inside. Her mother is watching television. An old Judy Garland movie. She's been crying, and her eyes are red. "Did you have a nice time?"

"Yes, Mum. We saw 'Batman.'" Her mother starts to ask questions, but Katherine interrupts. "I'm tired. I want to go to bed. Goodnight, Mum."

"Of course, *bambina*. We will talk in the morning. You go to your bed."

"Goodnight, Mum." Katherine shuts her bedroom door.

She changes into her nightie, gets comfortable under the covers, holds Pup. "I'm seventeen, and I've been kissed. I'm not the Beast tonight. Not tonight."

Chapter Ten

*K*atherine packs clothes, schoolbooks, the things she needs for the hospital. "Pup, don't sit there just because you're stuffed." She flings him into her bag. "Sorry, I'm in a hurry." She calls Jessie quickly to remind her to take notes for the classes she'll miss.

Katherine crashes into the kitchen chairs, bumping into Rachel who's eating toast and jam.

"Calm down, will you? I'll see you in the hospital in a few days." Rachel doesn't finish her breakfast. "I'll bring you something delicious afterwards. We can have a feast. You'll be all right. You always are in the end."

"Sure. Got to go." Her mother is waiting in the car. She's

not working today. Swapped her shift to be with Katherine, as always.

"Thanks, Mum." Katherine throws her bag into the back seat.

In the morning light, her mother looks pale. She switches on the radio as they drive towards the hospital. "Grandpapa and Nonna send their love to you." Changing gears, she changes the subject. "You lose too much time from school. If you miss too much school next year it will be hard for you to get into Medicine."

"I won't miss school next year. But this year I just have to have this operation and the other operations. You agreed, Mum. And ... there's the surgery on my face."

"I wish ..." Her mother hesitates. "You remember grafts can die ... and the Professor does not know if he can help you. There will be months in and out of the hospital, and there is the recovery ..." She takes in a quick breath. "You will be sick, Katherine."

I don't want to talk about it now. "Yes, Mum." *I don't care about being sick, I've been sick before, and the hospital ... it's part of my life. I can't imagine what it'd be like not going there. I want to look normal. Mum, I know you're worried, but I've decided. I have to try.*

Her mother chats lightly between songs playing on the radio. "Rachel is helping her friend Jill with makeup at a wedding. She enjoys doing it after the dental work." "Old Mr. Jones is still making his peas fly around the lunch room." "It was the right thing to give up the swimming. Study comes first, and your arm had to be fixed. You will be able to move much better after this operation."

Katherine answers occasionally, lapsing into her own thoughts. *I know you'll be there for me, for this and for the new operations, because I'm going to do it. Sometimes I hate the hospital. The surgery, being sick, the pain, the scarring, and when the grafts don't work. But the hospital means everything too, otherwise I wouldn't have long hair, I wouldn't be able to move my arm, or have normal breasts. It's just that I want more ... to be ...* She stares out of the window, searching for butterflies between the eucalyptus trees. It's been raining lightly. Early autumn rain. The leaves of the eucalyptus are glossy wet and beautiful. *I want to be Beauty. Not the Beast. Is that so greedy? After all that surgery ... can't I be Beauty?*

Katherine touches the side of her face. *The coach was so angry when I told him I wouldn't swim anymore. He shouted that I'd wasted his time, and I shouted back, "You wasted mine." Everyone heard. It was awful. I hate shouting, but do I feel bad about it?* She shakes her head. *No. He was wrong. I'm not a cheat. I just couldn't compete anymore.*

"We're here, Katherine." The hospital is large and familiar. Admissions. Forms to fill in. Details. Dates. Then corridors, nurses' stations, elevators. The ward is always the same. Katherine feels strangely comfortable as her mother waits to tell the nurse that her daughter has arrived. Katherine slings her bag onto the white-sheeted bed with the stainless steel

110

railings. *Home again.* She half-laughs. *No kookaburras and gum trees, but home.*

Katherine unpacks her nighties and personal things. Pup rests on her pillow. He's here for her, for every operation. She kisses him. "See, I still love you." *William said he'd visit. I hope, hope, hope he does.*

Her mother looks at the phone next to the bed, then writes down the number. The nurse recognizes Katherine. She jokes, "I'm not sure if I'm glad to see you or not. Well, you know what to do by now." There's her blood pressure and temperature to be taken, then more notes. Katherine's file is thick. Tattered pages mark well-used spots. "Split thickness graft applied posterolateral section of left thigh, immobilization of graft, scars more hyperplastic …"

"Onto the scales, Katherine." The nurse writes figures on the form attached to the plastic clipboard.

Katherine grimaces. *I hate this. Mum, don't you dare look.* The nurse writes down Katherine's weight, talking about the weather. "The rain's been a relief, hasn't it? You'd better change into this surgical gown. Not very glamorous, is it? The anesthetist will be in soon to talk to you. If you want me, just press the buzzer." She touches Katherine's hand. "Everything will be all right."

The process begins. Separation from life outside. Carts carrying medicines and reports rattle along corridors. Beepers shrill as doctors race towards emergencies. Break room gossip wafts between shifts. Flowers, visitors, food trays, gauze and bandages, patients … the hospital hive.

Her mother flicks through a magazine while Katherine looks out of the window at businessmen frantically rushing across the road, mothers pushing strollers, lovers walking hand in hand towards the park, derelicts slouching against the old walls of the hospital.

It's another life inside the hospital walls.

Books and colored paper lie across the tables. Children are seriously coloring with thick crayons. A young teacher is explaining a math problem to a fourteen-year-old boy. Half-hidden in a beanbag, a little girl with pigtails laughs at the story she's reading. Four kids are writing a play. An older girl stares out of the window.

A man comes into the room. He bends over the little girl in the beanbag and lifts her into her wheelchair. "Time for your physiotherapy." The little girl stops laughing.

In the morning, the children's ward is always busy. Children who aren't critically ill, but aren't allowed out of bed, play board games with children who are allowed. Some have assignments given by the hospital teacher. Kids with tubes in their noses, kids with drips attached to mobile units, kids with cancer and diabetes and cystic fibrosis and spina bifida play because they feel better today. Eight-year-old Katherine with no hair is drawing a picture of her mother and Rachel. Posters of the children's work are hung throughout the ward.

The nurses' station in the middle of the ward has a view of everything. Parents, nurses, doctors, social workers and teachers center on the children, who are the focus of a private world within the ward. Visitors come in from time to time bringing presents, and there are parties with balloons for birthdays. Mothers come in all the time, and the children get individual attention which their brothers and sisters don't receive.

Sometimes disturbing things happen there. Parents challenge the system. They argue with the doctors and nurses, guarding their children against decisions they question. The children are afraid then.

Sometimes terrible things happen there. Children get very sick. Some never go home.

Katherine cries after her surgery. The skin on her back has been cropped for her graft. It's red and throbs, and she vomits from the anaesthetic drugs. She calls for Mama, who holds her and stays throughout the night, and the nurses are kind, and all the people in the ward are kind. Even though it hurts, she knows she's special and safe because they all look after her.

The ward is her home.

The anesthetist arrives. Katherine refuses the pre-operative drugs that would calm her before she's wheeled into the operating room. The doctor discusses the procedures and fills in more forms before he leaves. "I'll see you soon."

Katherine lies on the gurney. Cotton weave blankets are tucked around her like a cocoon. Pup's under her left arm. The orderly jokes as he pushes her around corners and passageways, the ceiling whizzing past like on a roller coaster.

"Don't you think this is a Batman ride? I'm the Joker. Do you want to be Catwoman?"

"Catwoman? Maybe. I liked the Batman movie." *And William.*

Katherine's mother walks alongside her daughter like a guard against intruders, protecting Katherine from the onslaught of drafts and impersonal staff. They arrive. Heavy plastic sheets divide the operating rooms from the rest of the hospital. Her mother has special permission to go with Katherine into the inner sanctum.

The Professor is waiting. He's hard to recognize in his green surgical cap and gown, but Katherine knows it's him, with his thinning tufts of hair protruding from his cap and his eyebrows, which are white and bushy.

"Katherine, how are you?" His voice is concerned as he goes over the details once again. "Are you still happy to have the skin cropped from the back of your thigh? You know, we haven't taken skin from that section for a while."

"I know, Professor."

"Don't forget your arm will be in a splint when you wake up."

She half-smiles. "I won't forget, Professor. I've had a lot of practice at this." *So much practice, but I'm getting closer. Just a few more operations.* "What about my neck, my face?"

"We'll talk about that after this operation."

Katherine looks disappointed.

"I'm going to try, Katherine, if you really want it. If your mother agrees."

"I really want it." The anesthetist inserts a needle into the vein at the top of her hand. "That needle hurts." She hates the stinging liquid that burns into her hand, flooding her arm like molten lava. Her stomach knots, and the fears and memories she has before every operation erupt. She reaches out for her mother's soft jacket. Her mother presses her fingers against her lips. "I love you." Katherine starts to cry, but the tears lie quietly on her cheeks as she falls into unconsciousness.

Nothing. No time.

Fleetingly, Katherine opens her eyes. *Is it over?* She reaches for Pup. She sees her mother sitting in a gray vinyl chair next to the bed. *You're so young, Mama. Am I two? Six? Eight? Twelve? Fifteen? Are you young? Am I a baby? You're wearing the jacket.* Waves of nausea engulf Katherine. A nurse gently rolls her onto her left side, injecting an anti-vomiting drug into her thigh. The drip pumps fluid, salt, glucose into her vein. *Where's my arm? Have I got an arm? My leg. Where's my leg?*

Her mother's watching, helping, calming her baby as she's done every day for the past two months. Twice hourly, Katherine is turned by the nurse. Her small hands and arms and leg are mobilized gently. Katherine's pacifier falls out, but before she can cry the nurse pops it back into her mouth. Katherine's round face, with the feeding tube taped into her nose, momentarily brightens with a smile.

"You're beautiful, sweetheart, and I'm going to make sure

you can move properly and that you get better. I know you don't understand." The nurse strokes her cheek.

There is no pillow. Katherine lies stretched, her neck extended. The nurse rolls her over so she's lying straight. "You want to hold your head up high one day, don't you?" The nurse turns to Katherine's mother. *"She has to go for another treatment today to remove the dead tissue. You understand, don't you?"*

Katherine's mother is thin and pale. She whispers, "Yes, but is she getting better?"

"Yes, much better," the nurse answers softly, as she pumps painkillers into the drip.

Painkillers, nurses, her mother, doctors move in and out of Katherine's consciousness.

Then she's in the ward. Thick white dressings around her arm so she can't move it. Thick white dressings around her thigh where the skin has been cropped. Vomiting. Her mother brings water. Katherine passes water.

There are noises in the night. Night flashlights roam through the ward, people call out, buzzers, the nurse's face peering at Katherine. "Are you all right?" Katherine doesn't answer, shifting restlessly, moaning quietly.

In the morning, tea and toast. Katherine turns away. The drip is taken out. The outer dressing is changed.

The Professor checks the thigh for infection. "It looks good." He examines under Katherine's arm, looking at the dressing over the graft. "It all looks good, Katherine." *I don't feel good. It hurts. Everything hurts so much. I hate the hospital.*

Three days later Katherine's playing poker with an off-duty orderly. She's careful, awkward, but it's getting better.

"You're too lucky at this for me." He throws down his cards.

"Luck has nothing to do with it. I'm a great poker player."

He laughs. "All right. I've got to get to work now."

The graft under her arm is thick and swollen. Her arm is splinted, bandaged and immobile so that movement doesn't tear it. The back of her thigh is crusted over like a huge scab. Sore, but getting better, and Katherine's feeling happy. *Jessie's coming and Rachel and William. Where is my brush? Mirror? Great, I look like a ghost. I'll pinch my cheeks. That's better. Nightie. Ouch, my leg. Where's the blue nightie? Mum's always moving things. I can't stand it. Oh, there it is, in the cupboard. I like my nighties in the drawers, not in the cupboard. I'm glad Mum's back at work.* Katherine brushes her hair with her left hand, tugging at knots. She puts down her brush and runs her fingers along her shoulder, up her neck, through her hair. *I can't believe it, but Mum's said yes. Yes, yes, yes. She's the best mother. And the Professor's said yes. He said he can't promise it'll work, but it'll work. I'm going to wear my hair up one day. I just know it. I am. I am.*

"Hi." Rachel is standing there with an enormous chocolate Easter bunny. Jessie's next to her with a pile of schoolwork. William's behind them looking embarrassed, holding yellow, pink and blue snapdragons.

Chapter Eleven

*C*leansing with soap and water. The warm liquid seems to seep inside the tightness of skin and muscle, washing away the stiffness and pain of the night. Katherine half-listens to the nurse talk as the watery heat soothes and pampers. The young nurse tells her that she won her semifinal in the local squash tournament, and afterwards she went to a cheap Chinese restaurant with some of the team and her boyfriend. "We had a noodle-sucking competition. The soy sauce was all over everyone's faces, especially my boyfriend's. He was the worst." Katherine blinks, listening properly now. "He's hopeless. Can you believe he didn't even pay for my chow mein?" *William paid for my cake and coffee after the movies, except I don't know* *if he's my boyfriend. He didn't say anything when he visited with Rachel and Jessie. I suppose Jessie talked so much he didn't have a chance. He laughed when Rachel ate both of the chocolate bunny's ears. He doesn't know about my body, my face, my ...* Katherine raises her arm, rubbing under her hair.

The nurse grabs her arm. "Don't move. You'll pull the graft."

"Sorry. I wasn't thinking."

The nurse plies lubricating ointment over the graft. "I'll cover it after the Professor sees how it's healing. Onto your side. Is your thigh sore?"

Katherine nods as she maneuvers herself around, turning her back on the nurse. The nurse looks at the gauze mesh that was laid over the graft during surgery. The mesh is separating at the edges, which is a sign of healing. "There's no swelling. All the gauze will be off in another few days." Katherine winces a little, but she trusts the nurse who clips the mesh with her sharp surgical scissors.

"I've finished with the dressing, Katherine. Oh, I saw something for you at the nurses' station." She pushes the trolley loaded with its basins and gauzes towards the station, returning a few minutes later with a package. "Hope it's something nice."

"It's probably homework." Opening it, Katherine laughs. She's received a few of these packages lately – physics and math. "I'm right. Homework." The nurse grins as she goes to her next patient.

Dear Katherine,

"Come, come with me, and we will make short work."

I think the Friar's wrong, don't you? "Romeo and Juliet" wasn't short work, and this won't be either. But you must admit it was worth making the effort to understand Shakespeare.

I've put your next assignment inside this envelope. "to be byron. an anthology." There are some interesting new poets represented in this collection. Have a look at V.V. Sipos' poem, "to be byron." Her work is challenging, but you enjoy a challenge, don't you? We're all looking forward to you coming back to class and giving us your opinions. You always have a lot of them.

Get well soon.

Regards,

Mr. Roberts

Katherine flicks through the collection. *I can't believe it. There are pages and pages of poetry. Mr. Roberts, give me a break.*

The day is busy with physiotherapy, exercises, helping the nurses, phone calls.

Nonna calls. Katherine says a few Italian words to her to make her happy, but Nonna understands English. She's been studying English at a language school in Genoa. "So I can speak to my grandchildren properly," she says. "I am trying to teach your grandfather also."

"Are you *bene*, better, Katherine? Speak louder, *cara*.

Grandpapa is sending money to buy for you a pretty dress. You are not swimming your Mama tells to me. That is a great pity, but you will do this surf-lifesaving. This will be very good."

I can't wait until you visit at Christmas. Then we'll be like a real family. Money for a dress. Rachel will be so jealous. Jessie will have to come with me to chose.

Jessie's phone call: "You're so lucky you don't have a father. Dad went insane about Greg. Mum just hid in the kitchen as usual. She can't stand Dad shouting. Why can't I be like my good little sister, she's asking, no, *telling* me. Well, I'm not · my good little sister. Dad caught us in the car. We were only kissing. Who'd expect him to be snooping around at eleven at night? I hate him. Anyway, if he thinks I'm not going to see Greg, he's wrong. When are you coming home? I need a refuge. Well, at least on Saturday night."

Jessie, I don't know what a father is. The Professor's a father, and he is wonderful. Mr. Roberts isn't a father, but he'll be great when he is. I know that. There's Grandpapa who's far away. Mama says he is a good father. My father ... Rachel says before he left, he used to buy us ice cream. We'd eat it in the car, waiting for him to leave the pub. Is that a father? A dad? Sometimes I think I'd like to meet him. Ask him why he left Mum. Why he left us. Was it because of me?

Rachel's phone call: "It's a serious improvement not having towels and junk all over the bathroom floor, Katherine. The information on surf-lifesaving arrived. You have to do your Bronze Medallion to be allowed to get onto a patrol team. It looks hard. You've got to be in really good shape. I'll bring in the information today. By the way, some of your friends from the swim team called. I told them you're not in training anymore, but they want to talk to you. So you have to phone them. Jessie left some study notes for you that I'll bring in. That's it. So I'll see you tonight, then." *I'd be scared if you weren't around, Rachel.*

Her mother's phone call: "No, I have not forgotten. I will bring some paper and pens. What treatment have you had? The graft, is it healing? What about your leg? What did the doctor say about coming home?"

Questions, questions, questions. I love you Mum, but you give me a headache.

William's phone call: "I'm supposed to be studying, but I haven't done much of it. At least you've got an excuse not to. The surf's been fantastic on the peninsula. When you're out of there, maybe you'd like to come for a drive up the coast to have a look."

He called. He talked to me. He knows I'm in the hospital, and he doesn't care. Maybe he likes me. He's so cute. Will Mum let me go? Sure she will. Anyway, it's my choice. He definitely likes me. At least, I think he does.

Medication, meals, medical students' visits, dressings, blood taken, playing cards, night rounds and sometimes time to hide in a quiet corner. Katherine opens in the middle of "to be byron."

"theatrically he reads,
byronic, passionate,
a little sweat dripping
dropping insecurities
wiped clean on a handkerchief."

Katherine shudders. *I feel that. A Byron, but not a great Byron. Exposing your feelings to a crowd. Are we supposed to laugh at you? I don't want to laugh at you. I've sweated too. I think you're brave.* She closes the book. Another time, Mr. Roberts.

It's afternoon when her mother hurries in. She kisses Katherine and gives her the writing paper and pens she wants. "You look much better, *bambina*."

"I am, Mum."

Her mother consults the nurse over the treatments Katherine's had today, discussing her daughter's physiotherapy program and progress. She checks the time that the Professor will be in for his rounds before fussing around the drawers and bed tray. When she starts rearranging William's snapdragons, Katherine forces her eyes shut. *Stop it, Mum. Stop it. Leave my things alone. Go away.*

Katherine opens her eyes with a start when Rachel drops the surf-lifesaving information, phone numbers of the swimming team and Jessie's study notes onto her bed. Rachel laughs and drops the photo album she's carrying onto the bed too. "I have to tell you about last Saturday when I helped Jill on her wedding job. It was chaotic. There were five bridesmaids to do, as well as the bride."

"You should have been a beautician." Katherine runs her fingers through her hair. "You're good at doing hair as well."

"Only yours, Katherine. You'd never let anyone else touch your hair except me. Not even Mum."

A shiver runs downs Katherine's back. "That's true. I'd forgotten."

"Anyway, let me tell you about the wedding. I even got paid for it."

"What a showoff." Katherine laughs affectionately.

"Can you believe that Jill's asked me to help her with another wedding? All I had to do was put some touch up powder on the bridesmaids and thread sprays of white blossoms through their hair. My dress and hands smelled of jasmine. It was like being in Mum's garden except better because I heard all the gossip about who's going out with whom and what the groom does and the dating and everything. They must have thought I was part of the family." *Jill's Rachel's first real friend.*

Their mother leaves William's snapdragons and sits beside Rachel, next to Katherine's bed. Opening the album, they study the photographs. The bride is beautiful in her white gown of beaded satin and her flowing veil. The groom's eyes are glazed red by the flashing lights, or maybe by the shock of marriage and commitment. There are fathers and mothers and relatives and guests from generations of family and friends. Nostalgia fills the air between them as they share a family occasion that will never be theirs. A father, husband …

"Your grandparents will be here for Christmas," their mother reminds them, and they feel comforted.

"We have a family too, Mum." Katherine nods her head.

"Yes."

They're quiet for a while.

Rachel digs in her bag and pulls out some chocolate-covered almonds and nougat. "I brought these. Some of your favorites, Katherine."

She shakes her head.

"Just have one, Katherine."

"I'm not hungry. It's the anesthetic." But Katherine takes one to make Rachel happy. Rachel and their mother do too, and so do the nurse and the medical student who wanders in, and the tea lady who's announcing afternoon tea. It's a party. The med student tells rude jokes until Katherine's mother tells him off, laughing so much that everyone knows she doesn't mean it.

Everything stops for afternoon rounds. Hospital staff wait in anticipation. Patients look anxiously towards the door. The Professor is followed into the ward by a squad of students who peck after him like chicks, all jumpy and young, fighting for their rightful places. There is an understanding between the Professor and Katherine. She's an interesting case study for the students. The Professor has already briefed them on her history, and she's agreed to be "interesting." She answers the students' questions, lets them look at her scars and new graft, lifts up her hair when they want to see her hidden scars.

In return, the Professor sponsored her school work-experience program last term, where she followed him on his rounds, where he answered her questions, where she scrubbed up and watched him perform miraculous surgery. The Professor promised to help her try to get into medical school. He'll write a letter supporting her application and act as a reference when it's the right time. "But there are no guarantees," he says. *There're never guarantees. I know that.*

Secretly, Katherine believes the Professor is what all men should be like; what all people should be like. Secretly, she wants to be just like him.

"The surgical team is preparing for your next operation, Katherine. We've scheduled it for a few months after your midyear exams. You'll miss most of the remainder of the year."

"I'll make up for it."

"Are you prepared?"

"Yes, I'm ready." Both Katherine and her mother answer together.

Chapter Twelve

Katherine burrows under her freshly washed blanket. Autumn breezes drift through her window as she peers from under the covers. She can just see kookaburras on the empty clothesline. Growls bristle from the family room. Lions, wildlife special, her mother's favorite. Katherine imagines her mother warming herself in front of the fire, slowly drinking milky espresso from her handcrafted mug patterned with swirls of cream and sea green. There's a chip in the mug. Katherine had been only little when she knocked it over. She'd been playing ball with Rachel in the family room. "I'm sorry, Mama, Katherine sorry," her child's voice pleaded. Memory. Katherine hides under her blanket, trying to shake it away.

Her mother had been inconsolable, crying and crying. "Can't I have anything for myself? I am so tired. Tired. Can't I even have my coffee cup for myself?" Her words jumbled into sobs: "father," "alone," "hospital," "doctors," "alone," and Katherine and Rachel hadn't understood, cowering in the corner because their mother was always strong and brave. *I understand now, Mum. It's better now, isn't it, Mama?*

Rachel's CD player murmurs music softly as she moves around her room, putting out clothes for tomorrow. Katherine calls out to her sister, "Remember, you promised to give me a lift to school." *I've missed so much school, even with the extra work from the teachers. There are going to be so many things to catch up on. And I just know the swim team is going to be angry with me.*

"I won't forget, Katherine. See you in the morning." *Rachel never forgets anything, but I do. That physics assignment Jessie gave me in the hospital was hard. I couldn't remember how to do any of it. I'm useless.* Katherine grabs Pup. *Stop thinking. Go to sleep. I'm scared, that's all. I'm always scared going back to school after the hospital. It'll be OK. I'll be OK.* Carefully reaching for the bedside light, Katherine stretches her right arm. *That feels better. I can move. It's safe in the hospital. I'm safe at home, but tomorrow's different.*

As usual, Jessie is waiting for Katherine at the school gate. "Great to see you back. You've got to let me sleep over on Saturday night. I've told Greg I'm staying with you already, and I've got things organized." Jessie burbles on about her father and Greg and the physics assignment and Greg and school and Greg and … Greg.

Katherine interrupts. "Aren't you glad to see me?"

"Of course I am."

"I'm not sure. It sounds like you're just glad you might have a place to stay on Saturday night."

"That's mean. Really mean. You know Dad's been tough on me about Greg. I've been dying for you to come back to school. Anyway, I can stay at Liz's on Saturday night."

"You don't even know what tough is. I just came out of the hospital, remember?"

"You're so sarcastic, Katherine," Jessie huffs. "Sorry if I've said the wrong thing."

"I'm not sarcastic. It's just that you're pretty self-centered, don't you think?"

"No, I don't think." Jessie picks up her bag and heads toward the classroom. Refusing to look at Katherine, her blonde ponytail flicks from side to side as she stomps across the pavement.

Katherine walks behind her. "Come on, Jessie."

"Well, I was happy to see you, and it wasn't just because of Greg."

"It would've been nice to ask me how I am and maybe tell me what's been happening at school first. Slow down will you, Jessie?"

"No, I won't. I'm not self-centered. That's unfair. Who wrote notes for you at school? Who visited you in the hospital and brought the notes to you? Who phoned you every day?"

Katherine hesitates. "I guess, you did."

"Greg's important to me now, that's all. My dad's giving me a rotten time. I was going to ask you how you are, you know that."

"Will you slow down?"

Jessie stops suddenly. She's scowling. "All right."

"This is stupid, but I suppose I started it."

"You did."

"You know how I am when I come back to school after the hospital."

Jessie shakes her head. They stand there glaring at each other until Katherine bites her lip. "I was wrong. Sorry. Don't stay at Liz's. You know she drives you crazy with all her causes. She'll lecture you all night about being a vegetarian or saving the ants from extinction or something. You'll end up eating tofu, and you hate tofu."

Jessie puts her hands on her hips. "I don't mind tofu with chili sauce."

"Come on. Stay at my place on Saturday night. I knew I was going to be hopeless today. Sorry."

As Jessie heads for the lockers, she turns around to Katherine with a gratified look. "It's nice when you've done the wrong thing, not me. All right, I'll stay at your place on Saturday."

People call out, "Hello," "Glad to see you back," "You look great," as Katherine enters the classroom. The restless scraping of chairs against the gray linoleum floor indicates that Mr. Roberts is late, as usual. He dashes into the classroom, tosses his book on the front desk, looks around the room quickly. "I see you've returned, Katherine. I hope you're well and fit and ready to resume our study of literature?"

"Yes, Mr. Roberts. Thanks very much for all the work you sent me in the hospital." She rolls her eyes.

Everyone laughs.

"She speaks. O, speak again, bright Katherine, for thou art glorious to this class." Mr. Roberts picks up his poetry book. "Nice to have you back. I promise I won't make you 'speak' today. I'll give you time to catch up. The rest of you have no excuses. Now to the poetry of our bright, new poets. We'll begin with 'to be byron.'"

Books open, papers shuffle, pens are raised. Katherine has to share her book with Jessie. "Too busy planning Saturday to have your poetry, Jessie?" she whispers.

"Very funny. Shush, he's starting."

"'he's read before
alone at night,
his work unpublished
fingered in his desk drawer
but will they laugh
.... (at me)?

black collarless shirt,
tight blue jeans,

pub lights squinting
crinkled eyes
but will they laugh
…. (at me)?

he peers into the crowd
then down
at floorboards scratched
and splintered
i'm afraid.'"

Katherine listens for a while to Mr. Roberts questioning students about rhyme and rhythm, repetition, imagery, rhetorical questions: "but will they laugh?" "i'm afraid." The words circle inside her thoughts. She rereads the section, trying to stop the thoughts shifting inside her head. *It's all right to be afraid. I know what it's like to be afraid.* Katherine pushes her finger against the words on the page. *And guess what? Some people laugh. I've been laughed at. You've just got to keep trying.* Suddenly, she's perspiring. Beads of sweat collect under her eyes. She touches the wetness, then presses her hand against her right side. She senses the dryness of her skin even though she smoothed cream over her skin as she does every morning, every day, every week, month, year. *What have you been through, anyway? Nothing. How'd you like being called girl who has to hide? Hide in a paper bag? Where's your courage?* Katherine stands up. Jessie whispers, "Are you all right?"

"I hate this poem. Need some air."

"I'll go with you." Jessie starts to get up.

"No. Please, don't. I want to be by myself. If Mr. Roberts asks, just tell him I just need some air. Please, be a friend. Please."

Jessie nods uncertainly. "OK, if that's what you want."

Katherine leaves the room, moving past the desks, excusing herself to Mr. Roberts quietly. She sees him approach Jessie, asking if everything's all right. Outside the classroom door she takes deep breaths before walking along the corridor, climbing up the stairs, climbing ... climbing until she reaches the out-of-bounds rooftop. Out-of-bounds tobacco smells connect Katherine to the smokers and liars who always hide there. No one is on the rooftop now. She leans over the metal railing. The cold steel makes her skin goosebump, but her arms don't goosebump. She rubs her hand over her arms, rubbing, rubbing, but she can only feel the dullness of scars. She surveys the school, its old brick classrooms and new science building made of concrete and aluminum. A stretch of grass separates the buildings. Katherine stares at the grass scattered with clover patches and occasional white daisies.

Girls and teachers walk easily along the pebbled pathway, across the grassy lawn, to and from the old classrooms and the new science building. *It's easy for all of you, isn't it? You just walk on the path. There're no great, big potholes, are there?* Katherine watches the tops of girls' heads, some with ribbons knotted around braids, some with short hair that clings onto their scalps, some with blonde and brown and red and black hair. She flicks her hair back like Jessie would. *I'm so tired of potholes.* She hears a laugh as a girl runs into a classroom. Clenching the metal railing, Katherine suddenly calls out, "Unfair!" A few heads look up, searching for the voice, but Katherine jumps back, away from the railing so they can't see her. *Stop it, stop it, Katherine. I'm just nervous. It's the surgery, leaving the hospital, facing all the missed work. The stupid poem. That poet may be afraid to get what he wants, but I'm not. There is a path and it may be really hard to walk along, but I've decided. I'm not a coward. I've got things to do with my life.* She turns away from the railing, slides her feet against the concrete slab, pushes open the heavy fire door with its lighted *Exit* sign. There are other classes.

"Are you feeling all right now?" Jessie's relieved when Katherine joins the other girls on their lunchtime hill. Jessie offers her apricots.

"Yes." Everyone asks Katherine how she is after the operations, until she's annoyed. "I'm fine. Can we talk about something more interesting? Exams, for example."

There's laughing. "*Very* interesting."

"So when are you coming back to swimming? We lost the last relay," a teammate accuses.

"Come on, Katherine's been in the hospital, and she doesn't have to swim if she doesn't want to," Jessie defends her.

"Have you heard of free choice?" As usual, Liz leads the battle with heated arguments over who cares about swimming and school teams and rules.

"Thank goodness for Liz," Jessie whispers, nudging Katherine. "That so-called swimming mate is ignorant."

"No, I'm the ignorant one. Sorry about this morning." Katherine half-smiles. "I'm just going through my 'adjustment period,' as the Professor would say. That means I'm a bit confused. I'm better now. Totally confused."

They giggle. "No, I'm feeling OK now, Jessie."

"That's a relief. So can I tell you what I've organized for us?" Katherine nods.

"There's a concert on Saturday night that you have to come to."

"You're joking. I don't think it'll be very romantic, do you? The three of us. Greg, you and me."

"William will be there too."

"How do you know?"

"Don't ask the details, just thank me. He's going to call you."

"Jessie, you're too much."

"You mean, too terrific."

Katherine takes an apricot. "That's right. You're too terrific."

Chapter Thirteen

*K*atherine's mother puts down the receiver. Fiddling with her hair, she twirls it into wispy curls. She stares out into her garden. Suddenly, she turns away from the trees and their falling leaves. "Katherine, Rachel," she calls quietly. Then louder, "Katherine, Rachel."

Rachel emerges from her room, silver foils in her hair, but there is no sign of Katherine. The sound of rock comes from her room. Her mother knocks, then opens the door. Katherine's lying on her bed, studying English. Shouting above the music, her mother calls out, "I want to talk to you about something."

Startled, Katherine jumps up, then objects, but her

mother's voice is urgent. "Please, Katherine."

"All right, all right. I need a break anyway."

Rachel brings coffee and almond biscotti. She hands her mother her sea-green cup, puts the biscotti on the small table next to the couch, then settles into a chair, sipping her own coffee. Katherine takes a biscotti before she slumps onto the couch. They watch their mother pacing the carpeted floor between potted plants and chairs. She stops for a moment, stripping dry leaves and petals from her vase of roses on the mantelpiece. Leaning against the mantelpiece, her hands full of dying leaves, she faces the girls. "Your father called. He wants to see you both."

They stare at her for a while. Katherine edges back into the couch, trying to get comfortable. Then Rachel speaks, struggling with memories of him. "Why?"

Her mother shakes her head. "I do not know. It has been so long."

Katherine's quiet. *My father? What does that mean? My father? After all this time.* She bites her lip. *I don't remember him.* Playing with the edge of the old couch, she pulls out threads. *I don't know who my father is.* She wraps a long thread around her finger. "What was he like, Mum?"

She hesitates, then smiles at Rachel. "I have told you before. Young, beautiful, like Rachel." She coughs. "But too young to be married with children. Like me, too young. He liked the bush." Her mother closes her eyes.

I like the bush too.

They wait for her to continue.

"A geologist. That is a beautiful thing to be, working with the rocks, walking in khaki shorts and a shirt in the hot sun in the red deserts. He loved the outback of this country." She wipes her eyes. "Me also. He took me many times into the country, and we camped beside little creeks with rocks, and he made a fire to boil for his billy tea."

She whispers, "Then, I loved him."

"I don't remember that, Mum," Rachel says.

"No, he changed after the babies. Terrible changes. He did not like the city, and he had to wear a suit and go into an office." She hesitates. "We argued because he was late home, and he smelled of alcohol. Not the sweet smell of village wine after dinner shared with a family. Different."

Rachel leaves her coffee cup and biscotti to stand beside her mother. She puts her hands over her mother's hands.

"Your grandfather was right. He was different from me. I should not have run away with him. A stranger. Afterwards there were the burns, hospitals, everything … he left. I do not know why he wants to see you now. You must decide what you want." She presses the dried rose petals into the palms of her hands. "I cannot see him."

The cuff links on his suit reflect the hallway light bulb. His feet stumble along the floorboards, making shadows that darken the corner. The mother tucks the baby safely into her crib. "Shush, sleep, darling. Shush." Four-year-old Rachel clings to her mother's skirt. *"Rachel, let go of my skirt. You go to bed."* Nervously looking towards the hallway, her mother's voice whispers sharply. *"Rachel, you do as you are told. Let go."* The little girl cries, but her mother's hands are hard, forcing her into her bed with its Cinderella quilt and fairytale nightlight. Rachel is afraid of the dark. Shutting the door quickly, the mother waits outside the girls' room.

"What are you staring at?" the man asks roughly.

"Where have you been?"

"None of your business." Alcohol reeks from his breath. *"Get me some food."*

"Get it yourself."

"Cow." He stands with his feet apart. His heavyset build dominates the room as he saunters towards her and the girls' bedroom door. *"I'm saying goodnight to them."*

"You are not. You are drunk. They are afraid." She manages to turn the bedroom key before he pushes her aside, forcing her against the door so that the doorknob presses into her spine.

Their mother closes her eyes as she speaks. "You must choose if you wish to see him. For me, he is the past, and I must leave him there. He will telephone again." She goes into her garden.

Katherine loses her job at Cafe Smooth when she admits that she's having more surgery later in the year. "We're sorry, but it's just too much time away. We'll give you part-time work when it comes up."

"So Saturdays are free, and I'm broke," *and dependent*

again, Katherine complains to Jessie. Jessie's glad because she can come over earlier "to study," she tells her father.

Jessie's father usually works on Saturdays, but not this Saturday. He has a new car, and he drives Jessie over to Katherine's place. As he talks to Katherine's mother on the front porch, he sways his arms enthusiastically, expanding on his view of education, one of his regular topics. "It's important for the girls to do well in these exams. Education is the way to the top." He's slightly built like Jessie, but he seems bigger than life with animated arguments that impress Katherine's mother. When he notices Jessie shaking her head, he laughs. "Fine, I'm usually the one in a hurry, but I see you are today. I'll leave you girls with this one thought: When your teacher asks you, 'How were your exam questions?' I hope you've got a better response than, 'The exam questions were easy. It was only the answers that were a problem.'"

He dashes towards his car, calling out, "Study," before he drives away.

"Sure, Dad," Jessie mutters.

"Your father is right, Jessie." Katherine's mother picks up her trowel and spade, heading for her roses.

Katherine watches Jessie's father zoom down the street in his sleek sports car. Jessie turns away.

"People think Dad's great, but it's not like that. He puts so much pressure on me. Even if I don't have a boyfriend, there's no guarantee that I can get the grades he expects. If he knew I was going out with Greg tonight, he'd shout and Mum'd hide.

He gets so aggressive. It's his way or no way. I lie to him. I get scared that he'll catch me one day."

I lie to Mum sometimes, like you lie to your father. I don't want to. Mum pressures me. Makes me feel guilty, but I'm glad I have her. Are you glad you have your father? I know what a mother is, but what is a father?

Jessie follows Katherine inside. "We've got to do some studying. It's my deal with Mum. I can go out with William as long as I do my work first and," Katherine shakes her head, "as long as it's with a group. You and Greg are the group."

"Luckily, I like being a group."

"Honestly, how old does Mum think I am?" Katherine drags out her work. "I hope you brought the physics assignment."

They organize themselves in Katherine's bedroom with music playing in the background, Katherine on the bed as usual, and Jessie lounging on the floor. There are important discussions about the concert, Greg, exam nerves, surgery, William. "Do you think he really likes me, Jessie?"

"Boys are difficult to work out. He wanted to come to the concert with you. He came to the hospital, didn't he? So he likes you."

"Yes, but he doesn't really know me."

"Do you know him?"

"Guess I don't."

They open their books. Katherine slides off the bed to lie next to Jessie on the carpet. Notes, the assignment, books, are all carefully laid out in preparation. There's always a bit of initial nervousness when the deductive logic and analysis of science confronts them. Then they really start exploring the questions until they're engrossed in discovering scientific phenomena and answers.

When Rachel opens Katherine's door, they're surprised at how late it is. "Do you want to hear about my second wedding job today, or are you too busy studying? It was peculiar."

"We've finished, haven't we, Katherine? My brain's tired. It's nearly time for dinner anyway. So what happened?"

Rachel sits on the bed. "The wedding was in the park. You know, with a celebrant under a tree and birds twittering around."

"We get the picture, Rachel."

She smiles. "I love Jill. I was helping her give the final touches to the bride's and bridesmaids' makeup before the ceremony. There were these sudden gusts of wind. One caught the bride's dress. She looked like she was going to take off."

"Is that the peculiar bit?"

"No, just wait, Katherine. There was this dog, a brown-spotted mutt with yellow teeth. It got excited about the ballooning bride and started sniffing up her dress. She tried and tried to escape, but the dog kept sniffing until people started yelling, then chasing the stupid thing away. The mother of the bride was screaming to leave her daughter alone. The page boy spat his chewing gum at it, but the dog just ate it. The groom got so angry that he took off his shoe and threw it at the dog. Guess what? The dog ran away with it! The groom got married without a shoe."

"That's funny, Rachel."

"Jill and I laughed so much. I'm starting to think weddings are funny."

At dinner, the story of the dog gets wilder and wilder. The brown mutt now has ferocious teeth, and he digs holes the size of craters to trap the bride. The groom ends up throwing his jacket and shirt and trousers at the dog and running around in his underpants.

"This is getting as good as my stories at work," their mother laughs.

"You mean that those stories aren't true, Mum?"

"I am saying nothing," she grins, as she dishes out ravioli.

Dinner ends, dishes are washed, the kitchen is tidied, Jessie's changing into a dress her parents wouldn't approve of. Her mother takes Katherine aside. "You look pretty tonight."

"Thanks, Mum."

"But be careful about moving your arm too much."

"Mum, leave me alone."

"You are not used to going out."

"You mean in a group? It's about boys, boys. Just trust me, Mum. Don't worry."

"Katherine, you are only just out of the hospital. Does William understand that he has to be careful?"

"Am I a medical case?"

"No, of course not. It is not that. You do not understand boys."

"Are you talking about my arm, Mum?"

"Please, Katherine."

"It's because of my father coming back, isn't it?"

Her mother doesn't have time to answer as Jessie walks in. Her short maroon dress clings to her like plastic wrap.

"You look amazing," Katherine says, but her mother shakes her head. The doorbell rings.

"I will get it." Determinedly, her mother opens the front door. "Come in." It sounds like an order. Rachel escapes to the kitchen while Greg and William are pushed into the family room.

"Would you like a *limonata*?"

"No, we're OK." They echo each other.

"Come and sit down for a while. You are not in a rush, are you?"

"Well, the concert starts at seven thirty." Greg looks at his watch.

"Good, there is some time. I'll bring you the *limonata*. It is lovely with a lemon slice."

Greg goes over to Jessie. "You look great."

Katherine's mother returns with the drinks and gives one to Greg, then to William. "You will be careful, won't you? Katherine has not been out of the hospital for long."

William coughs as he drinks the *limonata*. "Sure."

"She will have more surgery soon, for more grafts on her shoulder and face."

Mum, what are you doing? Don't tell him about that. He doesn't know what I hide under my hair. Why are you telling him? Katherine glances at William, who's shifting uncomfortably in his chair.

"What do your parents do, William?"

"My dad's a plumber. He owns his business, and Mum does the accounts."

"So you want to be a teacher?" "Where do you live?" "Do you have a car? I hope you drive carefully." "What are your interests?" "Katherine has a lot more surgery to do." "I hear you like basketball." "What subject are you doing?"

Katherine looks towards the kitchen. Rachel is standing at the door. She calls her mother, "I need your help in the kitchen."

Her mother looks at Rachel for a moment. "Later."

Katherine tries to interrupt, but her mother keeps questioning. *Stop, stop. Who do you think William is? He's not my father. I'm not going to run away with him.* Katherine's screaming inside her head. *Stop, Mum, stop!*

Katherine elbows Jessie, who shrugs helplessly. *I've got to do something.* "Mum, can I have some more lemonade?" "Mum, we've got to leave." "Mum, is something burning?"

Her mother ignores her, bombarding William with more questions. "So you like surfing?" "How do you have time to study and surf?" "When will you bring Katherine home?"

Mum, he's going to abduct me. Can't you see? William is a blood-sucking vampire? Mum, please stop. But her mother doesn't stop. *I'll never forgive you for this. I've got to say something.* "Mum, we're going now, and we'll be back when it finishes."

Her mother starts again, but Katherine has already grabbed her sweater and her bag. "Let's go." She shoves Jessie in front of her. "We're out of here. Bye, Mum. Come on, let's go." Her mother follows them to the door, but they pile as quickly as they can into William's old Valiant.

Jessie and Katherine stare at each other before bursting into a laughing fit. They can hardly speak. "That was the worst."

"Horrible."

"Terrible."

William changes gears. He's quiet.

"It was awful." Katherine's nearly choking with laughter. "I don't know why I'm laughing ... it was so awful."

Jessie nods. "I've never seen that side of your mum." They both stop laughing.

"Me neither." *Me neither.* As the big old car turns onto the expressway, Katherine looks at William. "I'm really sorry. Mum's not usually like that."

"It was rough." William concentrates on the road, the radio blares, Greg's arm is around Jessie as they talk quietly in the back until they don't talk anymore.

Finding a parking space is difficult, as William's nineteen-year-old Valiant needs one and a half spaces. They end up driving around in circles until they find a spot in a dark alley marked, *No Standing.* "This'll do. Just right. I won't get a parking ticket. No one comes here."

"No wonder." Jessie looks around. "People could get mugged here. This is a dark alley, you realize."

"Don't worry, we're here. We'll protect you," Greg reassures them, and takes Jessie's hand.

Jessie pretends to hit his arm with her other hand. "You'll need protection in a minute."

"Come on, we'll be late."

"Do you go to the hospital a lot? I thought it was a one-off surgery this time." William asks Katherine about the new operation and the operations she's had before. She answers briefly, trying to change the subject. *I don't want to talk about this. You're going out with me, not a hospital case. How could Mum tell you about my scars? You can see enough of them anyway. I was going to explain things after we got to know each other, not right away. I thought you were going to choke on that drink when she blurted it all out. How could she?*

"I guess your mother's protective about you." Afterwards, William doesn't say anything more as he walks beside Katherine to the concert hall.

Say something. I can't. William, why don't you hold my hand? You did before. I want you to hold my hand. She glances at him, but he's looking straight ahead.

Inside the round building, thousands of people are jostling each other, searching for the right entrance door. Hawkers are selling hats and CDs for huge prices. "We go in here." Jessie hurries towards the entrance with Greg behind her. A lady takes their tickets and points to the ceiling. They start

147

climbing. "How far up are these seats?" Jessie asks suspiciously.

"Keep climbing. We'll get a great overview."

"You're kidding."

"Keep climbing. They were the only tickets left."

"I don't think there's much further to go unless we're sitting on the roof." Jessie pretends to pant. "Oxygen! We're here. It *is* the roof."

"Here's some oxygen." Greg gives her a long kiss. William and Katherine look away.

William and Katherine sit next to each other, separately. A low rumble starts moving through the crowds. "They're coming." Jessie leans forward. Lights start to flicker, the TV monitor glares, smoky gray puffs float across the audience. There are screams as the band surges onto the stage, grasping microphones, belting out electronic songs, crashing drums.

Music rocks the stage, filling the hall, reaching up to the ceiling. The crowds stand, swaying their hands, shouting. Jessie's pumping the air. Greg's pumping the air. William's pumping the air. Katherine pretends. *I'm not different, William. I'm like Jessie. See, I have long hair, but my eyes aren't blue like hers. They're brown. Do you like brown eyes? You kissed me. Remember?* Greg's arm is around Jessie. *But I'm not like Jessie, am I? I am different. I don't want to be. I don't. I don't.*

Chapter Fourteen

*W*illiam drops them all off at Katherine's house. He doesn't walk Katherine to the front door. Haltingly, he rubs his hand over the lambswool seat covers. "I'm surfing up the coast tomorrow. Meeting the guys at six. So I have to get going."

Katherine sees her mother is waiting. "Like a piranha," Katherine whispers, under her breath.

"The concert was great." Jessie nudges Greg. "I feel like a walk, otherwise I won't be able to get to sleep."

"I need a walk too."

"Do you want to come, Katherine?"

What would you do if I said yes? Sometimes your games

149

are irritating, Jessie. Just be honest. You and Greg want to be together, alone, outside, lying under a tree, watching the stars. I understand because I want it too, but who'd want it with me? "No thanks. I'm tired."

It's after three when Jessie tiptoes into the bedroom. Katherine has left a nightlight on for her. There is a mattress on the floor. Katherine holds her quilt close to her face so that Jessie doesn't know she's awake and watching her. Grass bits flake onto the carpet as Jessie unzips her maroon dress. It slides to the floor. Her skin is smooth, perfect. Jessie switches off the light.

Katherine stares at the empty black space. Under her quilt, she slips her hand onto her right side, ridged with scars and hardness. Crying quietly, she closes her eyes. Dreams make her turn restlessly in her bed. Fathers and mothers, William and hairy beasts crisscross the night, searching for the morning.

It's nearly midday when Katherine opens her eyes. Jessie's still sleeping. Katherine rolls onto her side, exhausted.

"Jessie. Katherine." The voice repeats their names again and again, nagging sleep away. "You must get up. It is lunch time already."

"Right, Mum." Katherine sees her mother open the door. She leans out of her bed and pushes Jessie's arm. "We're getting up." *I can't talk to you, Mum.* "You don't have to wait for us." She gets up and shuts the door.

Yawning, Jessie stretches her arms. "Best night. I'm so lucky. Greg's working out a lot for basketball, so he's really athletic."

"You came back pretty late."

"Yes, I did." Jessie hugs her pillow.

"I'm not going to ask what you did last night."

"And I'm not telling." Laughing, Jessie gets up. She grabs the towel Katherine left out for her. "Can I have a shower first?" Without waiting for an answer, she's out of the door and in the bathroom. Then there's the sound of water splashing and Jessie humming.

The afternoon consists of sandwiches and studying "Romeo and Juliet" and talking about last night. "I'm not really that interested in William." Katherine pushes aside a pile of papers looking for her poetry book.

"Why? I thought you liked him. What about his hazel eyes?" Jessie bites into a red apple.

The crunching grates on Katherine's nerves, but she ignores it and the lie. "He likes his car too much." *William doesn't want to go out with me. It's the operations. My burns. Mum.* "He hardly talked because he's more interested in surfing and fixing up his old Valiant."

"Guys and their sports and cars. Greg's like that too. Sometimes I think he likes basketball better than me. I'm lucky that he hasn't got a car yet." That starts Jessie on Greg, and the topic of William subsides into mild interest, then nothing.

"Jessie, we'd better get on with the poetry."

"One week, then exams. I think I'll do really well. Then I can tell Dad about Greg. I can't keep hiding him and don't want to anyway." Jessie opens the anthology of poetry. "Dad should be grateful for Greg. I've stopped partying since going out with him. What do you think?"

"Let's work, that's what I think." *I don't want to think.* Katherine reads aloud another of V.V. Sipos' poems.

"a girl
dedicates two months
to ritual stripping of flesh
in rites of starvation.
in the third month she'll leave
her core exposed
nowhere to conceal
inadequacies
parental desires
men defiling a Jewish grave
fairy penguins flapping oil slicks."

"That gives me the shivers. I don't think I'll ever diet again."

"You never do, Jessie." Katherine's voice is irritated. "The poem isn't about that. It's about being trapped by expectations, hopes, what you want to be."

"I feel trapped, Katherine. Dad expects so much, and Mum is so weak, she always agrees with him."

Will you ever understand how trapped I am, Jessie?

"I argue with them. Otherwise, I'd be like that girl. Nowhere."

Nowhere. I don't want to be nowhere. That's where I am. I have to talk to Mum. I have to.

They finish their work just as Jessie's father speeds up the driveway. Rachel opens the front door. "Your dad's here," she calls out.

"Coming. Is he still having fun with his new toy? I mean, his car." Jessie doesn't stop for an answer as she grabs her books and bag. "He hates waiting."

Katherine's mother chats to Jessie's dad through the car window until Jessie appears. "Thanks a lot for letting me stay. I appreciate it." Jessie climbs into the front seat. "And Katherine, thanks. You're a real friend."

There is waving and shouting goodbyes as the car disappears down the road into the last light of the day. Katherine turns to face her mother. "Can we talk, Mum? On the back porch?"

She nods. "Yes, I need to talk to you and Rachel too. Your father is phoning tonight."

Rachel follows them. The familiarity of the porch is comforting as evening settles over the house, the ghost gums, butterflies flitting among their mother's marigolds and roses. The wicker from the chairs is fraying at the edges. Katherine's mother takes out the shears she always carries in her apron pocket and cuts off the bits and pieces. "That is better." Reclining into the worn cushions, she waits until her daughters sit down. "Katherine, can we speak about your father first?"

"Why does he have to call us?" Rachel punches a cushion. "There's something wrong with this. It's too lumpy."

"Don't kill the cushion, Rachel." Katherine stands up and leans against the railing.

Their mother presses her fingers against her lips. She looks out towards the trees. "I have been hanging birdseed molds on the trees, and the rosellas have been pecking at them. Your nonna always throws bread onto the lawn for the birds, but it is not good for them. Seeds are better." She looks at the girls. "When he phones, I will speak to him, then you girls must talk."

"I don't want to Mum." Rachel hesitates, holding her cushion against her stomach. "It's too difficult. It took me a long time, but I've finally worked it out. I can't have those old feelings again."

Her mother doesn't argue. "If that is your decision, I will tell him. And what do you want, Katherine?"

I haven't worked out anything. I don't know what I want, what feelings I have. I know I'm angry at you, Mum, but him? Who is he?

Rachel interrupts. "He just left us, Katherine, when you got burned." Her eyes furrow into incomprehension. "How could he just have left?"

I don't know what happened. Do I want to know? Do I want to see him? I don't want to think about him now. It's too hard now. Later, Mum. Katherine runs her hand against the peeling railing. "This needs painting." White paint fragments scatter onto the floorboards. Katherine glances at her mother. *I've got to talk to you, Mum. How can I even start? Will you listen?* Images of the poet afraid to read his work, the girl stripping her body, shuffle inside her head. Katherine forces the images aside. *I've got to tell you, Mum. I have to. I'm not hiding.* "You know," she hesitates, "about William?"

"Yes." Her mother stiffens.

Katherine's quiet.

Her mother breaks the silence. "Yes?"

"I thought William liked me."

"Liked you? How? Did he?" her mother's accent sharpens.

"Did he?" Katherine repeats her mother's question.

"Did he," her mother stammers, "do anything?"

"Do anything?" *That's such a peculiar question.* "What?" Katherine stares at her mother, trying to understand. Then she recognizes something in her eyes. A look she has when she talks about Katherine's father, about men who are not Grandpapa. An accusing look. Katherine feels the blood rush into her head, and she's hot like burning. *Do you mean did he hold my hand? Kiss me? More?* She jolts at her words. She didn't know she was so angry. *Do you think he did anything, Mum? He didn't. He didn't speak to me. Didn't touch me. Who'd want to?* "No, William thinks I'm," she bites her lip, "ugly. He doesn't want me."

Her mother's face becomes pale and her eyes fragile. "That

is untrue. Katherine, you are …"

"Beautiful, I know. You've told me that since I've been little. I'm beautiful. It's just that no one else sees it." Lifting up her hair, she exposes the heavy scarring reaching down the side of her face and neck, vanishing under her T-shirt. "You told William about my scars, my face. Why, Mum? Why?"

"I did not. I cannot remember telling him."

Rachel looks at her mother. "You did, Mum."

Katherine moves next to her sister.

"Maybe I did then, but the burns are part of you, Katherine and …" Searching for an explanation, she looks pleadingly at her daughters.

"Not all men are my father, you know. Was he that bad anyway? What did you do to make him leave?"

Her mother's eyes fill with tears. Katherine doesn't want to see and turns her back on her. She leans over the peeling railing. "I don't know if I believe he was that bad."

"He left us. He hurt Mum." Rachel stands up. "And me."

"I want to protect you, that is all. Katherine, you are being unfair." Her mother hesitates. "And cruel."

Spinning around, Katherine protests. "Cruel? Mum, you don't want me to go out with William or anyone else. You made him see my scars, so I'll always be trapped. I'll be your daughter, Rachel's sister, but never me. You're always saying I'm like everyone else. I can have a life. Well, you showed me that I can't. I'm not normal."

"You are normal, better than normal. You do not understand."

"But I do. I want the operations so that I can try to look like everyone else. You don't want me to, do you?"

"That is not true."

"Stop it, Katherine." Rachel grabs her sister's arm, but Katherine can't stop.

"You want me to be your little girl forever!" Katherine's shouting. "Your protection's choking me. I'm grown up. I'm seventeen. Next month I'll be eighteen. I won't even be allowed into the kids' ward anymore. I'll be having my operations as an adult, Mum. An adult."

"Being an adult does not mean you are safe. Look at me. Look at all the mistakes I have made. I do not want that. I love you so much. These operations will not change you."

"They will, Mum. They will."

Katherine runs down the wooden steps into the garden. It's dark. She looks up at the sky. The last rays of sun have been replaced by an incomplete moon. *I feel cruel. I love you so much too, but it's not enough. It's not enough.*

Katherine bends over the roses. There are thorns. *Is that what life's about? Does everything always hurt?* She stares at the roses, as if they'll give her answers. A plain brown butterfly flutters onto a petal.

There's quiet. Katherine feels alone in the night. Her sister sits beside her mother on the porch.

Suddenly, her mother's voice startles Katherine. It seems to shriek through the flower beds and night stillness. "*Telefono. Telefono.* It is him."

Telephone? Him? What do you want from me, Mama?
Everything hurts. Hurts. Katherine leaves the brown butterfly
and the garden with its roses and thorns, climbs the wooden
steps onto the porch, avoids her mother's look and slides the
back door open. *I'm going to tell my father that I'll see him.*

Chapter Fifteen

*L*unchtime on the hill is windy. "Looks like autumn's arrived. We're going to have to have lunch at the back of the science building soon." Julia wraps her sweater around herself.

There have been exams all week. Katherine's last exam is today, but others still have history and geography to do. This afternoon's math dominates the conversation – questions, study notes, timetables. There is a nervousness in the talk. Even Liz worries about the questions rather than her campaigns – "Free Whales," "No Experiments on Animals," "Save the Rainforests." During the next vacation Liz is joining an expedition into the Daintree Rainforest. She's protesting against another four-wheel-drive track being hacked through the forest.

"Got to do well on these exams. There's next year too. It's pretty hard," Liz says.

"We're all doing it."

"I just have to make it into college, Katherine."

"And let me guess. What would you want to be studying?"

"Very funny. You know it's Environmental Science."

"You'll get in, if you want it enough. If it's important enough."

"It is." Her voice is serious.

Katherine nods. *You're like me, aren't you? You have your dreams, and so do I. I just have to make it. To med school. If I don't get in … I can't think about it. It's my mission. Mission impossible – it has to be possible.* Katherine listens to her friends sharing their aspirations and inadequacies. *Nothing's impossible. I like you, Liz. I like you, Jessie. I like all of you. No frightened poets here.*

They move reluctantly to the examination hall when the bell rings. "You'll be OK, Liz."

"So will you."

We'll all be all right. I'm not afraid.

Katherine smiles as they march like soldiers in line, down aisles. She doesn't smile when they have to break formation to sit at solitary desks. Rigidly, she touches the wooden desk, then looks behind at Liz, who mouths, "Good luck" to her. Teachers' instructions force her to pay attention. Exam booklets are placed facedown on desktops, pencils sharpened, pens checked, the commencement time marked in black ink on the whiteboard. "Turn your booklets over. You may start." For a moment Katherine stares at the whiteboard, the girls' heads bent down in front of her, the teacher surveying the hall. Opening the exam paper, she picks up her pen and writes her name on the top of the page. She grits her teeth. *I'm not afraid.*

One hour. Two students leave the examination hall. *They can't be finished already.* She looks sideways at Jessie, who's calculating answers on scrap paper. *Concentrate. Another two hours to go.* Touching her lips, she feels their wind-chafed dryness. Katherine takes a hard candy out of her pocket, licks it, rubs it over her lips, then sucks it. They're allowed candy for stamina. She focuses on the paper. Taking a breath, she starts working again. Time becomes irrelevant as problems are studied, calculated, resolved, until … last question. She puts down her pen. Rubs her fingers, smoothes the booklet. Relief drips through her mind. The clock shows ten minutes to go. Calmly, she checks her answers. She jerks her head forward when the teacher's voice booms through the hall. "Pens and pencils down."

Katherine is in the line of students who shuffle quietly towards the front desk. She hands in her paper. Outside the examination hall, there's release as they carry out the postmortem. "Tough paper." "Glad that's over." "I didn't know the answer to question three."

"Have to return a book. See you later." Katherine heads towards the library, chats to the librarian as she hands back the book. Gusts of wind buffet her as she makes her way out of the school grounds towards the bus shelter. The usual crowd isn't there, just a few stragglers waiting for the late bus. *Hope I don't have to wait for long.* Peering down the road, she imagines she sees a phantom bus. *No bus. I bet it won't be here for ages.* As she sits down next to an old lady on the bench, she notices some students standing on the other side of the shelter. She shivers. William is with them, his hands in his pocket, his tie undone, his brown hair cut short and close to his head. She looks down. *William, please don't see me. Hurry up, bus. No, he's seen me. Maybe he hasn't. He has. OK, OK. What'll I do? I don't want to talk to him after the other night. Ignore him. That's it.* She pretends to tie her shoelace, elbowing the old lady on the seat. "Sorry, sorry," she apologizes, as she stands up, half-crashing into someone else waiting at the stop. "Sorry, sorry."

"Hey, watch it. Why don't …" He stops mid-sentence. Awkwardly, he looks at Katherine. "It's you."

Marc. This is ridiculous. "Sorry, I'm bumping into everybody. Must be post-exam nerves." *What am I saying? I'm not sorry to you for anything.*

He mumbles, "Our exams aren't until next month."

"Well, that's my last exam." *Why am I speaking to you?*

"I didn't expect to see you here."

"I had things to do at school, so I'm late." She glances at William, who's looking at them. *You might be useful, Marc. You owe it to me. I'll never forget what you said to me. Hide in a paper bag. Guess what, Marc? I don't have to hide. I'm worth something. I have a body and even a mind.*

"So are you still working at Cafe Smooth? I haven't seen you there for a while."

Why are you interested? "I work there on and off. Depends." From the corner of her eye she sees William take his hands out of his pockets.

"It's a good cafe."

What are you talking about, Marc? William's still looking. I'll show you that I don't need you. You promised to take me surfing, and you didn't. You're such a liar. She moves closer to Marc.

"Would you … Maybe, you'd like to … What about coming to the surfboat races? It's a fun race, on Saturday afternoon. It's the last one of the season. A whole group's going. Looks like the weather will be all right."

Are you crazy or something? Has someone put you up to this? The bus pulls up. She picks up her bag and walks with Marc. As they pass William she smiles at him. "Hi there, William. Hope the surfing was great." *Hope it rained and rained.* Then she turns to Marc. "I'd love to go out with you next Saturday. Let's meet at Cafe Smooth, at around two." William and his mates follow Katherine and Marc as they board the bus. She sits behind the driver and puts her bag beside her so that the seat is occupied. "See you Saturday, Marc."

"Oh, right. So, I'll see you then."

The bus pulls up at Katherine's stop. She glances back at Marc and William before getting off. *That was so odd. What does Marc want? Hope William is jealous. He's probably not. Anyway, I don't care.*

Yellowing leaves grapple with dark green gums. *I like autumn, and it's my last exam today.* She smiles. *Last exam.*

Katherine looks for kookaburras on the way home, but only sees two magpies with brown-ringed eyes. *Better watch my head.* When she's entered their territory in the past, they've dived for her. She's had a few pecks. Spring is the worst, when they're protecting their chicks. *You remind me of Mum. I'll leave you alone*, and she runs towards her house.

Panting, she calls out, "Anyone here? I'm back."

Rachel slams her bedroom door.

"Are you still not talking to me?"

No answer.

Katherine throws her bag into her room. "Come on. You're never mad at me for that long."

"Well, I am now, Katherine."

"So you are talking to me." Ever since the argument on the back porch, Rachel has ignored Katherine. "I'm free. No more exams. What about a drive?"

Rachel emerges from her bedroom. "How are you going to get to the Bronze Medallion practice tomorrow?"

"You're giving me a lift."

"Maybe I will, and maybe I won't."

Their mother arrives carrying pizza. "Dinner is here. Not as good as what I make, but half ham and pineapple, half chicken." Katherine likes ham and pineapple, and Rachel likes the other. "Work has been busy with new people, and I am late. So it is takeout pizza tonight. I promise I will cook more soon."

"I'll make the salad, Mum." Rachel is already in the kitchen.

Katherine watches her mother put the pizza on the dining room table and place paper napkins beside three large plates. *I hate being angry at you, Mum.* Looking up, her mother brushes aside hair that has escaped from her bun. Her cheeks are slightly flushed.

"Are you tired, Mum?"

"Yes, I am tired."

Katherine gets three glasses and a jug of water. The family is quiet as they tear the pizza slices apart. "Salad, please," Katherine asks.

Her mother hands her the bowl. "Now that you have no more exam pressures I must talk to you, Katherine." She folds the paper napkin thoughtfully. "I am sorry if I did the wrong thing with William." Then she straightens the napkin, giving herself time to think. "You and Rachel do not know so much about boys."

"Mum, it's normal to go out."

"That is right. That is why you went to the dance."

"Yes, but you can't expect me to go to one dance, and that's it. Girls go out with boys afterwards. It could be William or someone else."

"I am worried."

"Well, don't be." Katherine shakes her head. *You want to protect me but* … "It's time to let go, Mum."

"Katherine, you do not know everything."

And neither do you, Mum. "You can't cross-examine everyone who takes me out."

"Is that what I do?" She looks at Rachel.

"Well, yes, Mum."

"I do not want that." She takes the paper napkin and rubs her hands. "I am sorry. Will you accept my sorry?"

Katherine is silent. *I guess I have to. William* … She looks at her mother's face with tears edging into the corners of her eyes. Katherine nods. *I accept your sorry, Mama, but it hurt so much.*

Rachel carries the plates to the sink and turns on the kettle. She takes out two mugs and her mother's sea-green cup.

Their mother takes a deep breath. "There is something else. Your father. Will you see him?"

Rachel shakes her head.

Katherine answers slowly. "Maybe. I've got questions."

"He can't tell you anything," Rachel retorts.

"Rachel, I need to work out some things myself. I want to see him." *You're pressuring me. Let me think about it, decide. Leave me alone.*

Her mother cups her hands around her sea-green mug. "I do not know."

Rachel stares at her sister. "Well, I don't like it."

"I don't like it here, Mama," Rachel cries.

There are six units on each floor. They're on the third floor. From their family room window they can see other buildings that look exactly the same as theirs. The hallway frightens Rachel with its graffiti and smell of urine. People come to clean it, but the next day it is the same. There are scary people living next door who scream at each other late in the night, but the yard is beautiful with pink oleander trees and a soft green lawn.

"We will not be living here for long." But she's told Rachel that many times. "We will have a pretty house soon."

It had been nearly a year ago since their mother left their home and their father. He'd been drinking and swearing. Her mother had packed the cooler with sandwiches, fruit, drinks, milk for Katherine's bottle. Her old car was filled to overflowing with clothes, pillows, blankets and the portable TV. The children like watching television when big, yellow teddies run around in their checkered shirts. Rachel has her own yellow teddy that she cuddles when she goes to sleep.

They fled from their house in the suburbs – leaving friends, school, familiar shopkeepers, the local Catholic church with the cemetery attached. They didn't have much money and nowhere to go. In the inner city the welfare worker was kind. The emergency accommodation would only be temporary, she'd said.

Later, their father came to find them and banged on their door and frightened them. Rachel and Katherine hid behind their mother. He said he wouldn't pay any money, and he'd see them when and how he wanted.

The welfare worker visits and talks to their mother in the yard. Seven-year-old Rachel is running after Katherine, who's giggling. The gardener working near the oleanders has piled the green garden leaves and clippings in the square brick pit. He throws firelighters and gasoline into the leaves because they're still too green. Striking a match, the garden refuse catches quickly. He waits until the fire is well established before going to collect the other bundles of clippings to add to the fire. Gas pools on top of the uneven bricks that encase the pit.

Katherine's pacifier drops onto the grass near the pink oleanders. She bends to pick it up and turns to her sister who's calling her.

Rachel sings, "Katherine is a bell. Ding, ding, Katie, Kate."

"Rachey," the baby voice gurgles, then she runs towards the pretty red and yellow flames near the oleanders. "Rachey. Pretty, pretty. Rachey."

Screaming. Screaming. Scream …

"Katie! Katie!" Rachel runs to get her mother. Then the mother's running, the gardener's running, the welfare worker's running. Rachel stands still on the lawn, crying.

Chapter Sixteen

The Patrol Captain calls out, "Go!" Sand scatters madly from under bare feet as racers charge across the beach towards the surf. Red and yellow caps disappear between plunging waves as they splash furiously out to sea. Conditions are windy, with the waves coming in quick succession. Katherine struggles against a dumper with its tremendous force. She loses control as it throws her against the underwater sandbank. She sees another swimmer tumble too, but Katherine recovers quickly. She looks out towards the horizon. Her arm is free since the graft, and with the strength of her swimming training, she speeds towards the colored buoys. She makes it past the breaking waves, racing towards them. Three other swimmers are with her. Her arms ache as she splashes around the buoys, then heads back towards the beach. Quickly assessing the waves, she catches a big one that carries her past two other racers. Her feet hit sand, and then she runs as fast as she can through the shallow water, tearing from the water onto the sand, sprinting to the finish line between the two flags. As she gasps for breathe, the Patrol Captain calls out, "Second. Good one, Katherine."

She looks towards the pool, imagining herself standing on the blocks. Waiting for the starting gun. The anticipation, the tension, the dreams. *Do I miss it? The teammates? The repetitive laps, up and down, up and down. The coach? No.*

Surf racing is quick – pounding arms and legs, splashing, diving, catching waves, bodysurfing. Surf racing is smart – understanding surf conditions, weather, wave formations, tides, currents. Surf racing has a purpose – training lifesavers to keep beaches safe.

The Patrol Captain addresses Katherine as everyone packs up flags, the rescue reel, the equipment. "Can I talk to you afterwards? At the clubhouse?"

She glances at the plain brown brick building that holds the club's boats, surf skis, boards, rescue equipment. She thinks of her swimming coach and instinctively covers her arms and shoulders with her towel. The Patrol Captain is occupied already, checking equipment and procedures.

At the clubhouse, the surf patrol swimmers jostle each other teasingly. There's discussion in the locker room about training for the summer Surf-Lifesaving Championships. Katherine waits in the game room for the Patrol Captain who is talking to a boy. When he notices her, he waves. "Just a minute, Katherine. I have to tell my son something."

Katherine pulls her T-shirt over her wet bathing suit while she waits for him to finish. His hands move with his words as though they are part of his speech, reminding Katherine of her mother. There is something big in the coach's movements, even though he's a short, stocky man. He tousles the boy's hair before sending him to the locker room.

"Thanks for waiting, Katherine." He runs his stubby fingers through sun-bleached hair. "I can see you're a good swimmer, but I think you've got a bit more than that in you. You've got a feel for the surf." Rubbing his chin, he speaks seriously. "I'm training a team for the Rescue and Resuscitation Championships. It's tough. A six-person team. A rescue is simulated. It's got to be fast and technically professional, with a beltman, reel team, lifesaving techniques in the water and on the beach." He stops. "There's a lot to it. Are you interested?"

"I'm interested." She hesitates. "But I have to have some surgery this year. I won't be able to swim really until next year. I can only train on and off for now."

He thinks for a moment. "You have to do the theory anyway first, for your Bronze Medallion. You have to learn how to keep someone alive. There's plenty to learn. If you're not ready for this year's competition, there's next year. The surf-lifesaving association is more than a sport."

She smiles. "I'm coming to see the surfboat races this Saturday."

"Good, I'll be there too." He nods. "So you'll train with us until the surgery and start the theory. When you're ready, you can join the team."

"Yes. I'd like that."

Pleased with her answer, the Patrol Captain puts his hand on her shoulder, with its grafts and scars. Surprised, she doesn't jump back, but just looks at his stubby fingers. *Can't you see my burns? Doesn't it matter?*

"I'll see you on Saturday." Then he pats her on the back with a strong, firm hand, like a father. "You'll be a great lifesaver. You're a good kid. A good girl." Warmth filters through her mind as she leaves the clubhouse. *Good girl.* The words ignite memory. *Did my mother say that to me? My grandpapa? My father? Daddy?* All of a sudden, she shivers. *I want to be a good girl, Daddy's good girl. I want the Professor, Mr. Roberts, the Patrol Captain, to think I'm a good girl. Even Jessie's dad. I want my dad to think that about me.*

Katherine heads for the parking lot steps. Rachel's meeting her there. "Thanks for coming to get me. I know you didn't want to. I'm going to like surf-lifesaving."

Rachel's voice is sharp. "Great."

"Come on, Rachel. Don't be angry."

"What do you expect? I haven't forgotten what happened the other night." She refuses to look at Katherine. "And I

172

know you're going to see him."

"Come on. I'm not doing this against you and Mum. How could I? I couldn't stand it without you. I respect your decision not to see him. All I'm asking is for you to respect mine."

Rachel shakes her head as they walk towards the car.

"I have to ask him about things. I need some answers, that's all. Maybe I won't see him again afterwards. Maybe I will. It has to be my choice. I can't just do what you and Mum say anymore. Please understand."

"*You* try to understand. Mum has done everything for us. He hurt her. He'll just hurt you too. We don't need him. Not now."

"I've got to find that out for myself." They get into the car. "Please, I don't want to argue. Rachel, smile, will you? Do you want to come to the surfboat races on Saturday?"

No answer.

"You've got to start speaking to me again because it's …" Katherine's voice falters. "It's hard without you. Please, Rachel. Please."

"You're so stubborn." Rachel looks at her sister for a moment. "It's hard for me too." She hesitates. "All right, but I still don't approve."

"I don't expect you to."

The tension between them eases as Rachel drives, concentrating on gears and pedals. Rachel hates being angry at her sister.

"The car sounds great," Katherine exaggerates, then starts explaining surf-lifesaving. "It's better than competition swimming. You patrol the beach and save people's lives. You need to get a Bronze Medallion to patrol, which I don't know much about yet. And there's the greatest competitions like Beach Flags which sounds boring. It's not. It's wild with everyone diving into the sand grabbing for a baton. There are belt races, beach sprints, relays, board riding, surf-ski races. I really want to try that. I'll get to paddle on a surf ski right over the waves, and there's the ironwoman challenge …"

"Stop, stop." Rachel throws her hands in the air. "If you tell me one more thing I won't come with you on Saturday."

"Hey, keep your hands on the wheel or you'll kill us."

"Frightened you, didn't I?" Rachel smiles as she takes control of the steering wheel again. "Don't worry, I'm an excellent driver."

"That's what you think." Katherine laughs. "But about surf-lifesaving …"

"I'm warning you, if you don't want an accident, let's get onto something else."

"All right." Katherine gulps down a laugh. "I've got interesting news. Do you remember Marc?"

"How could I forget him?" She shudders.

"Well, you won't believe this," Katherine pauses for effect, "Marc is the one taking us to the Saturday surfboat races."

"You're kidding!"

"I know it's crazy. Maybe I should stand him up. Should I?"

"Why are you bothering to go with him?"

"It's to do with William." Her eyes light up. "And Marc as well."

Rachel shakes her head.

"I bet you thought William was in love with surfboard riding and that's all? Wrong. Can you believe that I'm in the middle of a love triangle?"

"No, I can't."

"Well, I am." Katherine gives Rachel a seductive look. "Actually, Marc's been trying to meet me in Cafe Smooth and on the bus. He's even tried to get friends to plead his case because he is so desperate for me." Katherine yawns. "It's just exhausting, chasing him away. Now, Marc is in real trouble because of William, who's the main threat in the battle to win the heart of Beauty. I'm Beauty, if you haven't worked it out yet."

"You're giving me a big beauty of a story, Katherine." Rachel prods her sister.

"Just listen. It gets romantic now."

"I can't wait."

"William, the brooding surfer, has to decide between me and his surfboard. He just loves that surfboard, all smooth and wet. William slides his bare chest over the smooth board. His body shimmers in the hot sun."

"But it's autumn. Nearly winter!"

"Shush. William presses his muscular body against the board itself. Riding the big, waves, he pushes hard, torpedoing ahead."

Rachel's laughing.

"It's the ride of love with all its twists and turns."

They're both laughing now. Rachel pulls up in the driveway, switches the ignition and lights off. Katherine is trying to open the car door in between bursts of laughter.

"Hold on, Katherine. Stop laughing." Rachel waits until they both calm down. "I still don't understand why you're going anywhere with Marc."

"I told you. It's the love triangle."

"Be serious, Katherine."

Katherine tries to interrupt.

"Can you listen? Katherine, listen. This is important to me. To us."

"What is it?"

"I don't care about Marc, your love triangle and your games. But I care about ..." She looks at her sister. "I don't want him ... you know, our father ... to come between us."

Katherine shakes her head.

"If he came between us, it ..."

"Rachel, I promise he won't. He can't." She touches Rachel's hand. "No one ever will."

Katherine has already had several appointments with the Professor. He has ordered some pathology tests in preparation for the surgery. On Saturday morning Katherine goes to the blood collection center. She lies in the chair which welcomes her with its soft gray leather. Sighing, she extends her arm. It's routine, automatic. The nurse rubs the arm with alcohol. It's cold. Katherine turns her head away as she always does. The fine needle pierces her vein like a sting. Three vials of blood today. It's always a relief when the nurse removes the needle, and Katherine can press the cotton against the pierced skin. Sometimes she doesn't press it hard enough, and her arm bruises into a blue and purple patch. The nurse puts on a circular bandage.

Katherine is meeting Rachel at Cafe Smooth. She crosses the road to go through the park, one of her favorite walks. Leaves flood the paths in the last days of autumn. The roses are just stalks and thorns. Their flowers have wilted into pods. *Why am I seeing Marc?* Katherine picks up a white petal, pressing it. *Marc's like a bruise that's sore that I keep pressing, even though I want to stop.* A possum with curious brown eyes stares at her, then scurries up a tree.

Katherine waves at Rachel, who is sitting on one of the director's chairs outside.

"Have you had your blood taken already?"

Katherine drops her bag on the table. "It's nothing." *I don't want to talk about that.* "I've just got to say hello to the cook first."

Katherine is back in a few minutes.

"That was quick."

"Quick? Right." Katherine drags out another director's chair, then stares distractedly along the sidewalk.

"The dental office was so busy this morning. It was hard to get away. So these boat races had better be fun."

Katherine doesn't answer.

"Are you listening?"

"What? Listening? Sure I am." *Why am I meeting Marc? I'm pathetic going with him after what he called me.* "This could be a mistake."

"It's a bit late to tell me now. Anyway, I thought Marc was desperately in love with you?"

"Not so sure about that." *I don't want to go.*

"Well, why am I here?" Rachel shrugs. "This cappuccino is terrific. Really creamy. Do you want one?"

Katherine looks around nervously. "Does this black top look OK? Oh, it doesn't matter anyway, it's only that idiot Marc."

"I take it that you don't want a cappuccino?" Rachel bangs the table lightly. "Can you hear me? If you've changed your mind about this afternoon we can just tell Marc to get lost. Or do you want to leave? We can go now."

Just as Rachel says that, Marc appears. He's wearing a Manchester United cap, blue jeans and a white sweater. "Hi. Are you ready to see the game? Should be a good one."

Rachel looks questioningly at Katherine. "Are we going to the surfboat races, then?"

I don't know. This is humiliating. Katherine gets up. "I guess so." They all leave Cafe Smooth together.

Katherine glances at Marc quickly. *You're good-looking. I*

know you don't think I am. Why am I here? Marc discusses the skills of trying to row against the waves. "It'll be a rough one because the wind is up."

They meet some of Marc's crowd at the beach. Rachel sees a girlfriend, and she joins them.

"Lots of people here. I'll be in that team next season." Marc offers to get Katherine a drink before it starts. Katherine and Marc head for the kiosk. They don't talk. She tries to, but it's as though a cork has plugged her throat. She coughs repeatedly.

"Are you OK?"

No, I'm not. What am I doing here with you? What am I trying to prove?

It's Marc who breaks the silence. "Do you remember that day at the bus stop? At the beginning of the year?"

How can I forget? You made me cry.

"You know, afterwards Jessie told me off."

Jessie? She never said anything to me.

He coughs too. "As soon as I said that to you, I knew I was pathetic. I was showing off." He takes off his cap and stops. "Jessie was right. I was … gutless. I've been trying to get the courage to tell you ever since. I saw what you thought of me at Cafe Smooth that time we met. I went there on purpose to see you."

I can't believe this.

"I don't know why you said you'd come with me today. I thought you'd stand me up."

I nearly did.

"I'm sorry. I hope you can forget I ever said those things that day. They are stupid and untrue. I am sorry. Sometimes, I'm a real jerk."

"Yes, you are."

Chapter Seventeen

The surfboat races seem to mark the end of autumn as winter winds and rains arrive. Jessie and Katherine walk quickly into the school grounds.

"You didn't tell me about it, Jessie."

"Are you angry?"

"I would've told you not to say anything to Marc." Buffeted by the growing storm, they start to run. "Let's get inside." They hurry up the stairs into school.

"But are you angry?"

"He told everyone that no one would ever want me, that I'd have to hide in a paper bag." Katherine's steps slow down as she stammers. "Somehow, it doesn't hurt as much since

181

Marc's said he's sorry." She touches Jessie's arm. "It doesn't hurt as much since I know you defended me. No, I'm not angry."

They hear nervous chatter coming out of classrooms.

"Grades and results today." Katherine pretends to smile. "You'll do fine, Jessie."

"So will you, Katherine."

The day is strained, as windows are closed to stop rain coming inside, and as teachers hand back papers. There are arguments from students afraid of their parents' judgments or upset by their own careless errors and unprepared questions. There is excitement too, with high marks and good grades. Liz is ecstatic over a B in math. "My worst subject. Now I'm ready for the rainforest expedition."

"Rain is right. I don't know about the forest, Liz. How can you go when the weather is like this? How can your parents let you?" Julia's voice is miserable as she throws her D geography paper on a desk.

"I'm not a little kid, so they can't stop me, but why would they anyway? They know it's important to me."

Looking over Jessie's shoulder, Katherine puts her hand on her back. "I knew you'd do it. A first in physics. A grades in everything else, except English. B+."

Jessie flourishes her exam papers. "After Dad sees this he's going to have to back down about Greg."

"Greg. Greg. Even a first in physics is just an excuse to go out with him. You're out of control." Katherine recites, "Greg.

Greg. 'What's in a name? That which we call a rose / By any other word would smell as sweet.'"

Jessie pretends to hit her. "Ha. Ha. So, how did you do in English?"

"Not bad. Eighteen out of twenty for my 'Romeo and Juliet' essay. A."

"Who's got the name of a rose now? Mr. Roberts?"

"That's a piercing observation, Jessie."

"No, a fragrant, sweet one, I'd say."

Katherine moans. "That was awful."

"You started it, Katherine."

Everyone is discussing results when Liz interrupts, "Guess what?" No one stops until Liz is shouting, "Are you listening? Party! Do you want to hear? Party."

Conversations end. Partying is interesting business. "My parents said that if I passed everything I could have an end of term party." Now Liz has everyone's attention.

"You have terrific parents." "When?" "What time?" "Casual?"

"Is it a tofu party?" Jessie teases. "Oh, yes, and I can wear my slinky black vinyl skirt."

"You'll be gorgeous as well as saving an animal, so what are you complaining about? And we might have some chili sauce for the tofu."

"Hey, who told you about the tofu?"

Liz ignores Jessie's question. "The party's next Saturday. Eight o'clock and definitely casual. Everyone's invited."

They play around, teasing each other, joking, letting the pressure of the past weeks disperse into talk of Liz's party and vacation. By the time the last bell of the day rings, the rain is pelting down. Some girls linger in classrooms, hoping it will ease. Others brave the weather. Cars line the road, disrupting traffic as parents wait for their daughters. Umbrellas buckle as some of the girls make a dash for the bus shelter.

It's late by the time Katherine fights her way home. She's cold. *Heater, heater.* Fumbling with controls, she switches it on. *Hot shower. I can't wait.* As she opens the bathroom door, the vitreous green bathtub seems to stare at her. Katherine always shudders when she sees it. She never has a bath. Rachel has endlessly tried to explain the luxury of soaking in warm, steamy water on a cold, miserable day. She's never persuaded her. Katherine has stopped repeating to her, "I'm afraid of the hot water." "I'm afraid of not being able to get out." She can't explain her vague memories of stainless bathtubs and burned skin, doctors and nurses. She turns on the shower until watery mist fogs the bathroom and is seeping under the door through the house.

"Lovely and warm in here." Stripping off her raincoat, her mother carries it to the laundry room. She asks Rachel to put her umbrella on the porch, then calls out to Katherine, "*Bambina*, how did you do in your exams?"

Katherine emerges from the bedroom in her warm navy

sweats. "Fantastic. Terrific. But what can you expect?"

"There was so much terrible noise-music coming from your bedroom I was not sure, Katherine."

Rachel shakes her head. "How are we going to live with her now? She'll be showing off all night and all day if I know Katherine."

"Will not. I can't help it if I'm a …"she twirls around in a pirouette, "genius."

"In your own mind."

"Obviously I don't get appreciation from my very own family."

"You are appreciated." Her mother smiles. "So what marks did you get?"

The gas heater radiates comfort through the family room, making the room intimate. The wind shaking the branches of the gums outside seems distant. They look through exam papers until there's nothing more to say. Rachel doesn't mention that she passed her dental technician exams. It doesn't seem important when compared to Katherine's results.

Discussion turns to the events of the day. "Liz is having a party. Rachel, you're invited."

"That will be nice, to go together." Their mother smiles as she listens to Katherine talk to Rachel about what to wear and who is going.

When they've finished their party talk, their mother speaks. Her voice is serious. "Katherine. The Professor's receptionist called today." She speaks quietly, and Katherine and Rachel lean towards her to hear. "Katherine's operation has been scheduled. The Professor wants to see us next week."

Katherine shivers.

"Are you all right?"

"Yes, Mama." *Excited, nervous, happy, scared. I want the operations. I want them.*

After dinner, when the girls are washing the dishes, their mother can't wait any longer. She pours coffee into her sea-green cup and carries it to the family room chair. Placing it on the small table, she glances at her daughters before lifting the receiver to seek reassurance from halfway across the world. "Katherine has done very well, Mama, in her exams … The operations will mean missing a lot of school, but she should have it done. *Si, si,* yes, she will have to catch up on her studies. Maybe she will do another semester at school … You will see her at Christmas looking even better … Katherine will love the knitted bed jacket you made for her to wear in the hospital."

Katherine calls out, "I'm not wearing a knitted bed jacket."

"Do you want to speak to her? Katherine, you can finish the dishes later. It's your nonna."

Taking the receiver, Katherine whispers to her mother, "I'm not wearing that bed jacket."

Her nonna is interested in her school grades and the surf racing and the operations. Grandpapa talks for a while. Then Rachel talks before handing back the receiver to their mother, who has so much to say and so much to hear.

The last days of term are filled with tidying desks, making vacation plans, returning library books. For the last English classes, Mr. Roberts shows the video "Tom and Viv" about the life of T.S. Eliot and his wife Vivien Haigh-Wood. "If you thought, V.V. Sipos' poetry shows indecision, then you haven't read T.S. Eliot. I'm looking forward to exciting discussions about his poetry next term."

Jessie nudges Katherine. "Mr. Roberts is always excited, but I'm more excited that T.S. Eliot is the last poet we're studying for the year."

"Come on, Jessie. It'll be interesting." They settle into seats in the audiovisual room.

Sprawling country homes and green English pastures splash the affluence of the British upper class across the screen. So different to gray-brown bush and wild surf. Katherine is fascinated by Viv, who's wonderful, crazy sometimes with a wild intellectual eccentricity that challenges society's rules. Viv falls in love with T.S. Eliot who is conservative, inflexible, doesn't smile. Katherine elbows Jessie. "Why does she love him?"

"She's in love with his poetry, not him, if you ask me. Now shush, we'll miss the next part."

The film disturbs Katherine. Eliot's increasing rigidity makes him incapable of sympathizing with Viv's moods. But he uses Viv's creativity to write his poetry. In the end, his oppression drives her to insanity, and he commits her to a sanitarium.

"That was terrible. Is that what men can do to you?"

"Men like him. But look at Greg. He's …"

"Sensitive, kind, wonderful. Please Jessie, can we leave Greg out of this for once?"

"No, because there are lots of guys like Greg. It's ridiculous to say all men are like Eliot in that film. They're not. Otherwise why are we always talking about them, wanting to go out with them? You like William."

"Well, that ruins your argument, doesn't it?"

"No. You mightn't like William anymore, but why are you coming to Liz's party? Is it only to be with the girls?"

"Yes."

"I don't believe you."

Me neither. It's all confusing. "That film has got into me." *What's wrong with me?* "So, I'll see you on Saturday night? With Greg?" *My father called. That's what's wrong with me. I'm meeting him tomorrow.*

"See you at the party."

Saturday. Katherine waits until Rachel's left for the dental office. Only then does she get ready to leave. She lies, "Mum, I've got some casual work at Cafe Smooth today."

"It is very bad weather. Do you want me to drive you?"

"No, Mum. It'll be all right. I'm meeting … umm … some girlfriends on the way." Katherine hurries out of the front door before her mother can ask her anything else. *I hate lying to you, Mum. What else can I do?* The rain has stopped, so Katherine detours along the bush track. At first she walks slowly between the wattle trees with their spindly branches and smooth green bark. They've lost their summer flowers, and their leaves seem dark and barren. She grabs at the narrow leaves, then kicks aside branches that have been blown onto the muddy track. She starts to walk quickly. *He'll be waiting.* She starts jogging. *I've got to get it over and done with.* Then she's running so fast that mud splashes on her shoes, and the trees blur into the background. The stitch in her side forces her to stop. *I don't want to stop. I want to run, run,* but she leans against a mountain gum with its rough gray-brown bark, waiting for the pain to subside. *I've got to be calm. I wish I'd told Mum.* She tears at the peeling bark, exposing its creamy white trunk. *No, I don't.*

As she leaves the bush track to reach the road, she sees the corner cafe with its sandwich board out front: *Open.* It starts to sprinkle with rain again, so she hurries towards it. She notices a kookaburra sitting on the power lines above. *I hope that means good luck. Or are you giving me a warning?* The cafe smells stale, as if it's been there too long. A reddish-haired man is sitting at a table. He looks up. *Blue eyes, different to mine.*

Standing, he smiles at her. Katherine doesn't smile. *You look like the photographs in that album. Do I recognize you?*

"Katherine. It's been a long time."

What will I call you? Dad? Father? Papa? No, I'll call you nothing. "Hello."

"Do you want something to drink?"

"Cappuccino, please."

They sit down at the table. He orders two coffees, then looks at her. "You've grown up."

Yes, I'm grown up. All grown up. A tingle goes down her spine. Confused, she stares at him. *Why don't you know that I'm grown up?*

"How have things been?"

"All right." *Really hard.*

"What have you been doing?"

I don't even know where to start. Do you want to know about yesterday? Last year? Ten years ago? "Studying a lot."

"How's your mother? Rachel?"

"They're all right." *Mum's doing a fantastic job at work. Rachel's a dental nurse, and she's studying to be a dental technician.* Katherine smiles to herself, *and she's great at making braids.*

The coffee arrives. Katherine watches his thin lips on the rim of the bulky white cup. He's a tall, heavyset man. A good-looking man. His hands are big. *You could have protected us, made us feel safe.* He says he's still a geologist and works in the outback, the Kimberly, for a mining company. He hasn't been back to Sydney for more than ten years.

She stares at him, trying to recognize who he is, what he means to her life, what she's searching for. *You don't know anything about me, do you? The Professor knows my burns, and that I want to be a doctor. Mr. Roberts knows I love literature.*

190

Jessie's father knows I'm his daughter's friend. Even the Patrol Captain knows I want to do surf-lifesaving. What do you know?

"I know it's been a lot of years," he stammers, "but I'd like to see you, Katherine. And Rachel."

"Why did you send me birthday cards?"

He speaks slowly. "Because you're my daughter."

Daughter? I don't know what that feels like. What is it? "I don't understand."

His words are careful, quiet. "I drank too much when I was with your mother and you girls." He looks into his coffee cup. "There's no excuse for it, but there are reasons. I didn't like the city. Having kids. It was too much responsibility. Afterwards there was your accident. I wasn't ready. I'm sorry about things."

Sorry? Is that why you're here? "Mum had to do everything by herself. You hurt her."

"Yes. Your mother was young, pretty, clever, a good mother."

"She's still a good mother. Someone I can trust." *Not like you. You just left us? You didn't like the city. Having kids. Me being ... Am I supposed to say it's OK? Rachel hates you.*

"I'd like to talk to your mother and Rachel, and get to know you."

Why? Get to know me? What about all those years before? You left. Mum didn't even have her family here. She had to do everything. There were some friends who helped us. Doctors who did surgery, but it was Mum ... "I don't know."

"I'd like to make it up to you. I feel bad about what I did."

You're joking. Suddenly, Katherine stands up. *Do you want me to forgive you? Say it's all right? Make it up? Can you ever do that?* She stares at him, trying to recognize what she's been searching for. *Who are you? A stranger.* "Why didn't you help us? Why? You're my father."

He shifts uncomfortably on the green vinyl seat. "Please sit down, Katherine."

No, I don't want to. She watches him squirming. *I want you to squirm. You could have been someone important in our lives.* "I'm burned, you know."

"I know." He pushes his seat away from the table to stand up.

"You say that, but if you really knew, why didn't you stay? *It's been hard. Mum and Rachel and I have made it alone. There have been so many operations and the burns ...*" Katherine stops breathless, as if she's winded.

"You don't understand, Katherine."

Pressing her hands against her stomach, she stares at him. "I do." *You never visited again after I got out of the hospital.* "I wanted a father."

"I am your father."

I understand now, Rachel. I understand.

Chapter Eighteen

*T*he music blares through the small, seventies house. People crowd into the rectangular family room which extends from the open kitchen. Katherine looks at her watch for the twentieth time. Eleven o'clock. She leans against the canary-yellow pantry cupboards, fashionable in the seventies, but glaringly outdated today. The brightness is oppressive, and Katherine turns away from it.

She sees Marc with a few mates. He said hello to her when she arrived, but she didn't want to talk to him. A shiver tingles down her back when she notices William with a girl. Turning away, Katherine looks at Rachel chatting with a group of friends. Rachel spent hours ironing her blue jeans and red top until they were creaseless. This time it'd been Rachel who'd asked, "Do I look all right?"

"You look great, Rachel." Through the glass doors, Katherine glimpses Jessie and Greg on the back terrace. Jessie's wearing a thick beige sweater over her bright pink skirt. Katherine can just see Greg's arm around Jessie.

Corn chips, hummus, nuts, salsa, avocado dip are scattered on tables throughout the room. "Pizzas are coming soon," Liz announces, as she whirlwinds through the room.

The bathtub is filled with ice and drinks. Pizzas arrive. Vegetarian, cheese and pineapple, anchovies and mushroom, double cheese pizzas line the counter. Everyone descends into the kitchen, around the counter, grabbing and pushing until Katherine is squeezed like toothpaste into the hallway.

I want to go. Jessie's father is driving them home, but she knows if she phones her mother she'll come now. *You're always there, Mum, aren't you? No one else has been.* She thinks of the afternoon, meeting her father in the cafe. It makes her cringe. *When will this party end?*

She's startled when Liz grabs her arm. "Come on, we're throwing Julia."

"Throwing Julia? What?" Katherine is dragged into the circle. Even though the rain is beating against the windows, the room is hot and stuffy. Rhythmic music establishes a hypnotic pulse. Cans are thrown to the floor as hands are raised. Julia climbs on top of the hands, screaming when there's a dip, screaming when there's a high. Jessie climbs up, her pink skirt edging up her thighs. Leaning on a few guys' shoulders, Greg climbs up too, so that three of them roller coaster over currents of movement.

By the time Liz turns down the music, everyone's sweaty and laughing. Taking a six-pack of drinks, Marc and his mates sit on the back terrace. Someone puts on a slow song and dims the lights. Jessie and Greg are hardly moving as they sway in each other's arms. Rachel is dancing with Liz's older brother.

"Do you want to dance?"

Katherine doesn't answer as William takes her hand. She can't think. He puts his arms around her, and she leans against his chest, shuffling slowly with the music. *What did I expect from my father? What could he have said to me? Sorry? That's not enough.* William is talking to her. *What are you saying? You don't want me. I'm too ugly, aren't I? A hospital case. Are you dancing with me as a joke?* He holds her close. *You're so warm. I wish you cared about me. I wish someone did. Why didn't you ask me out? You promised.* Suddenly she's angry, really angry. She looks into his hazel eyes. *I like the color of your eyes, but I don't like you.* "Why didn't you take me surfing?"

"Surfing? Umm … it was only … for the guys."

"Why didn't you ask me out somewhere else?"

He shifts uncomfortably. "I wanted to."

"No, you didn't." She speaks quietly. "It's because of my burns." *That's why my father didn't want me. You're the same.*

He stammers, "That's unfair."

"Is it?"

"Yes, Katherine."

She moves out of his arms.

"I've had to study. There's the surfing too." He hesitates.

Katherine shrugs her shoulders. "Sure."

"All right. Do you want the truth?"

"Yes."

"It seemed too … tough to go out with you. Your life's … complicated. I wasn't ready."

Katherine shudders. *Ready? Ready for what? Don't say that. My father wasn't ready. Ready, ready …*

"I wanted to go out with you." He gently pulls her back into his arms, and Katherine feels she can't pull away. "I think you're special. You're smart, interesting and … pretty," he stammers. "OK … will you go out with me?"

Go out with you? How can I? She doesn't answer. Focusing on the music, she's quiet as they move in time with the rhythm. Other couples dance near them, holding each other. Jessie and Greg are kissing in the corner. Katherine leans against William's shoulder, grateful that he doesn't speak.

As arranged, Jessie's father arrives to get them at one in the morning. They run out to the car. "Don't want Dad to come inside," Jessie whispers to Katherine and Rachel, as they get into the back seat.

Jessie diverts her father with descriptions of the party until they reach Katherine and Rachel's house. Before driving away, he waits until their mother opens the front door and waves.

Rachel drops her handbag into her room, then goes to the

kitchen to put on the kettle. "Mum, Katherine. Do you want hot chocolate and cookies?" Rummaging through the cookie jar, Rachel shakes her head at her sister. "Someone's eaten all the good ones."

Katherine feels too disturbed to go to bed. She slouches into an old armchair next to her mother and sister around the heater. Rachel talks about Liz's brother. "He's nearly finished his apprenticeship. Building." She stammers, "He asked for my phone number."

Katherine feels surprised. She's never thought about Rachel going out with a boy. She's exhausted, and listens to Rachel and their mother talk about the party, friendships, a promise of a promotion for Mum, grandparents visiting. She says a few words here and there, cocooned in the intimacy of three women. *I wish I could tell you about my father. I don't know what he means to me, but he's not part of my life. You are. You're my family.*

Katherine sips her hot chocolate. Winter means that her mother's roses and jasmine, kangaroo paw and birds of paradise, are missing. *Birds of paradise. Flowers called birds, as though they're flying with their orange wings and blue tail.* Curling up into her armchair, Katherine thinks to herself. *I wonder if William likes me.* Getting more comfortable, Katherine looks at her mother and sister. *I'm home.*

Home. Rachel runs and runs around the backyard of her home. Katherine follows her like a mummy, bound up in her elastic suit.

Their smart, neat lawn is mowed regularly by government workers from the Department of Housing. On the back porch there are clippings from friends' gardens and seedlings growing in small plastic pots waiting to be transferred into soil. "I have to prepare the garden beds first." Their mother has already dug trenches along the side fences. Overlooking the back fence, there is bushland. Two eucalyptus trees are inside the backyard fence. Katherine points excitedly to a kookaburra.

"We can hang pots of seeds from the trees for the birds, Katherine."

They each have their own room, but Katherine shares with Rachel. She's afraid of the dark and cries if Rachel doesn't sleep with her. After Katherine's accident, they got priority for a cottage from the Department of Housing.

"Thank you, Mama. I love this house." Rachel hugs her mother and Katherine chases the kookaburra.

The Professor walks towards them as Katherine and her mother enter his office. His eyebrows furrow together. "Come in. Come in." He points to two chairs, then pulls out his chair from behind the desk. He sits down, shuffles a little in his chair, then carefully begins to explain the procedure of transfer of skin and tissues to the face, neck, shoulders; the cutting out of scars and distortions. Katherine listens to the medical jargon she's heard since she's been a little girl. He speaks softly. "It will be painful, and you have to be prepared."

Her mother looks at Katherine.

"I am."

He leans his chin against his hand. He points to a diagram, discussing the details of the procedures. "Am I being too technical?"

I don't want to listen to clinical explanations of skin and grafts today. She looks up at the Professor's framed diagrams of miracles. Her mind wanders, dreaming about putting her hair into a high ponytail like Jessie does.

"The surgery is delicate. Remember, this is only the first stage. Afterwards I'll need to refine the shape and texture. So there'll be a number of operations on the neck, the side of Katherine's face."

Katherine touches the right side of her face.

He pauses. "Katherine, I want to be honest. There are no guarantees. You have to be prepared for a rejection of the tissue and imperfect results."

"I trust you."

"Please don't. Katherine, I can only promise to do my very best."

Katherine's mother is quiet as they make their way to the car. Katherine asks her what's wrong.

"Nothing is wrong. I am thinking about the new operations. It will be easier than when you were a little girl. You are older. You understand more." She hesitates. "I hope you will not be disappointed." She brushes aside her daughter's hair. "Even if it does work, it may not be as you imagined."

"Mum, I've had disappointments before." She puts her arm through her mother's. "But you've taught me hope. If it doesn't work this time, I'll try again. It will work in the end. I know it will."

"You are beautiful the way you are."

Katherine smiles. "So you keep telling me." She gets into the car. "Let's go. Rachel's taking me to the surf clubhouse tonight. Don't want to be late."

"No, we won't be late."

Rachel drops Katherine at the clubhouse. "I'll be back in time to get you." She's meeting Liz's brother for coffee, and she's nervous.

"Real loyalty. A date's more important than supporting my training." Katherine hugs her sister. "Don't be late to pick me up, or you'll have to tell me every, disgusting detail of the date."

Rachel drives away, leaving Katherine walking towards the clubhouse. The Patrol Captain is already there, organizing fitness programs for his patrol. Katherine watches his hands. They seem to encompass everyone as he instructs some on techniques, others on surf awareness, everyone on fitness. She waits until he sees her. "Do you remember that I've got to go into the hospital?" she stammers. "It'll probably be a few months before I can get back here. Is that all right?"

Katherine's thankful that he doesn't ask about her surgery.

He just accepts it. "There's the theory I told you about before. I'll give you a training manual tonight. It'll start you on the way to getting your Bronze Medallion. You need it for patrolling the surf and my Rescue and Resuscitation team. You can call it R & R because you're nearly a team member, aren't you?" Smiling, he points to the rowing machine. "Today, you can work out with the others. Fifteen hundred yards on the rower, then the treadmill. Say another fifteen hundred. Then weights. You have to maintain fitness over the winter. The open sea isn't a place to begin a new fitness program. I've seen lifesavers in trouble when they do that. But you won't get into trouble. You know where you're going."

She straps her feet into the rower. Grabs the wooden handle, then pulls hard, straightening her legs as she jerks it out, bending her knees as the chain contracts. Pulling, straightening, pulling … *Know where I am going?* The Patrol Captain's words repeat in her mind as she looks ahead. Katherine enjoys the rhythmic movement of her arms pulling, releasing, pulling, releasing. "One, two, one, two, one, two," she counts to herself, until she's in a familiar routine, and her thoughts are free. *Where am I going?*

Chapter Nineteen

ighteen. How do I feel about it? Grown up? Afraid? Picking up Pup, she hugs him. *Mum wants to give me a party. I just can't have one before the operations.* She looks through the presents she's been given. Some CDs from Jessie, a wildlife book from Liz, some soaps and bubble bath from other girls. *Nonna and Grandpapa sent me one hundred dollars. I'm going to save that for vacation.* Looking out of her window, she tries to see if there are any buds on the trees. *No, it's still winter. William asked me out for my birthday. He did kiss me once, but if he touches me now, after everything, I don't think I could stand it.* Katherine hugs Pup again. *Don't worry, I'm supposed to be too complicated for William. Complicated? He means my scars.*

But they're part of me. He'd have to touch them. She shivers. "So, Pup, you're my only boyfriend after all." She kisses his patchy head.

"Ready?" her mother calls out. "The restaurant is booked for seven thirty. We do not want to be late and miss the show."

"Coming." Katherine throws Pup onto her bed.

"After this show, you will not listen to your rock music anymore."

"Sure, Mum."

The doorbell rings. "I'll get it." Rachel opens the front door. "Wow."

"Someone likes you," the delivery man says, as he waits for her to sign.

Rachel looks at the attached note. "They're not for me."

"Don't worry. The next one will be." He whistles as he heads for his truck.

"I don't want the next one." She hands Katherine the posy of pink roses intertwined with maidenhair fern.

To Katherine,
Happy 18th Birthday
from your father.

Their sweetness makes her gag. *He's sent me another birthday card. Flowers too.* She puts the flowers into the kitchen sink. "They're from him." She doesn't look at her mother.

Her mother walks up beside her. "The flowers are pretty."

Her accent softens the words, as she speaks. "Eighteen years old." She pauses. "Eighteen years is a lifetime." Fleetingly, she places her hand over Katherine's. "You make your own decisions now about your life. I will always be there, but it is time." She glances at Rachel. "What is important is that we are together."

"Thank you, Mum." Katherine kisses her mother.

Rachel taps her watch. "Come on. We'll be late if you keep standing there."

Katherine leaves the pink roses in the sink. "What type of place are we going to, anyway?"

"You'll see. Let's just go."

The restaurant is crowded. Guitars, old LP records, sheet music, 60s' music posters, leather gear are plastered over the walls. The waiter's black hair is slicked down with gel except for a lock of hair hanging over his forehead. "Stud," Katherine winks at him. "Elvis reborn." The waiter shows them to their seats.

"This is a crazy restaurant, Mum." Katherine looks at the plastic menu folder. "But great food. Pasta and pizza. I want ham and pineapple, of course."

As the lemonade is served, their mother takes a special bottle out of her bag. "Your grandfather sent this celebratory wine from the village. *Sciacchetra*. It is white and sweet. We always had this with our family meal at night."

"Elvis and sciacchetra," Katherine teases. "I thought you disapproved of drinking."

"Too much, that is very bad. But this is your grandfather's gift for tonight."

"And I'm eighteen now."

"You are eighteen." Mama kisses Katherine. It sparkles into their glasses. "To Katherine," Rachel toasts her sister.

Rachel produces a small package wrapped in paper covered in pictures of pups.

"Pup is my true love, after all." Katherine smiles.

"This is from Mum and me, as well as Pup."

Katherine opens the card:

To my daughter Katherine,
You were a beautiful baby, and you are still beautiful. There have been so many battles to overcome in your life, and you have been remarkable. Thank you for being special. You have a wonderful future.
I love you always,
Mama

To Katherine,
Now that you're eighteen you're old enough to keep your room TIDY, but more importantly, keep the BATHROOM tidy. You never know who'll see your undies lying on the floor there. It mightn't just be Pup. Apart from that, you're the best sister anyone could have.
Love,
Rachel

Slowly, Katherine unwraps the puppy dog wrapping. "I want to keep the paper." Inside, there is a dark blue velvet box. She strokes the velvet before opening it. Rachel and her mother lean towards Katherine, shutting Elvis and the restaurant out of the moment.

"It's lovely." She lets the shining gold chain hang from the palm of her hand and holds the finely engraved pendant. Three small diamonds are encrusted in the top of Katherine's initial. "I love it."

"Each diamond is to remember our family – one for your mama, Rachel and you." Her mother puts it around Katherine's neck.

"I love it."

Suddenly "Elvis the Pelvis" blasts onto the floor. "Love me tender, love me true …" His crystal-studded white vinyl shirt is unbuttoned nearly to the waist. Tight white pants and a big black-buckled belt. A girl at the next table screams, "Elvis we love you!"

The pianist dressed in black leather gear accompanies Elvis who pivots wildly around the tables. "Oooohhh. Come on sweetheart … Love you aaalll."

"Heartbreak Hotel," "Wooden Heart," "Suspicious Minds." Elvis belts out songs, and the audience joins in, singing, cheering. Elvis serenades the girl who screamed out at the start of the show. "You know that I'll always love you." He leaves her swooning and turns to Katherine. Taking Katherine's hand he kneels at her feet singing, "I'll always love you."

Katherine blushes, and her mother blushes with her. Rachel takes out her camera when Elvis sings "Happy Birthday." A cake with twinkling candles is brought out by the Elvis look-alike waiter. The whole audience sings "Happy birthday to you" until Katherine's blushing, and she blows out the candles.

"What did you wish for?" Rachel nudges Katherine.

My secret.

It's one of those nights where everyone joins in the rock and rolling, around tables, singing into the pianist's microphone with Elvis, who is gyrating his hot hips. At two in the morning, the restaurant finally closes, and everyone calls out goodbyes as if they're old friends.

The three women walk arm in arm down the street, singing "Since my baby, baby, left me ..."

Katherine touches the pendant around her neck. "I'm happy."

Lunchtime is photo time. Katherine shows her friends photographs of the "Elvis the Pelvis" night on her camera.

"Is that really you singing into the microphone, Katherine?" Julia giggles.

"You have no idea what a terrific voice I have," Katherine jokes.

"Mum is a great dancer." No one can believe that Katherine's mother is rocking and rolling with the Elvis look-alike.

Jessie taps her feet. "That's a different mum to the one I know." She laughs. "Your mum is always so," Jessie stops tapping, "responsible."

Responsible. That's Mama. Looking after us. Katherine holds the photo tightly. But she was young for my birthday. Like a girl. Not responsible. I love her being young.

Jessie elbows Katherine. "More photos."

"Sorry," Katherine flicks through lots more. "There's Elvis when his sideburn fell off. It was bushy. Found it in the salad. I thought it was a caterpillar." Images of her old scalp make her smile. "Don't worry, I didn't eat it."

There are moans and groans, until Julia starts on a story about her discovery of half a worm in her apple. Then the moans escalate. "We don't want to hear your story, Julia." But she wants to tell it.

"You're not a vegetarian anymore," Jessie laughs.

Before she can answer, the bell rings. Lunch is over. "Saved by the bell," Jessie says, as she puts her arm through Katherine's. "Sounds like you had the best eighteenth."

"I did, Jessie."

They are in class when a room monitor speaks to Katherine. "I've been looking for you. The Senior Coordinator wants you in her office. Now. You know the rotten mood she gets in if she's kept waiting."

"What's it about, Katherine?" Jessie asks.

Katherine shrugs. "I don't know."

The Coordinator's door is half-open. Katherine peers inside.

"Hello, Katherine. Come in. Come in. How are you?"

"Fine."

"Good. We've got a lot of things to discuss and prepare. Sit down." Adjusting her metal-framed glasses, she indicates the other side of her desk. "I need to write to the Education Department regarding your operations. I will arrange to stagger your exams over a number of terms, so that you're not penalized when you miss school later in the year. There are concessions we can get for students like you. Your mother is ethnic too. Italian. That's good, and a sole parent as well. All that helps." She fills in forms while she speaks. "Concessions for students with special needs."

Special needs? Katherine jerks forward, scraping the aluminum legs of her chair against the floorboards. *Special needs?*

"All right. Let's begin." The Coordinator starts reading out questions. "Name. Age. Address. Mother's name. Language spoken at home. Disability. Katherine, how old were you when the accident occurred?"

Disability? "Three."

"I need medical records. Who is your current doctor? What hospital? When was the last operation? When are the new operations proposed? Your mother is a sole parent. She's working now? Where is that?"

Disability? Special needs?

Katherine is five, running around in her elastic suit with a piece of soft yellow foam wedged under her right arm to stop webbing. She doesn't like the "sausage" and lets it fall to the ground.

Her mother picks it up, calling out to Katherine, "Come here. Come here, now."

She doesn't, and her mother has to chase her until Katherine's running. "Stop, Katherine," but she doesn't, running faster and faster, laughing at the game. Her mother is puffing and red when she catches Katherine. "You are a naughty girl. This isn't chasings," but Katherine giggles and blows big kisses.

"You are a naughty girl, but I love you so much." She strokes Katherine's round, flushed cheeks. "Please be good. Don't throw the sausage away. You upset Mummy. You'll make me cry. Do you want to do that?"

Katherine shakes her head. "No, Mama. No sausage."

"You need it to get better. You're my special girl, and when you wear this it makes you even more special."

Katherine's face scrunches into a frown. "I don't want to be special, Mama."

When the Coordinator finishes her questions and has filled in as many papers as she can, she says to Katherine, "Go back to class. You shouldn't miss more classes than you have to. You and your mother will have to sign some forms later."

Katherine stands to leave, then hesitates. "I'm not. I'm not disabled, you know."

The Coordinator looks up.

"I won't sign anything that says I'm disabled."

The Coordinator takes off her glasses. "But you have some difficulties."

"They're only skin deep," Katherine answers derisively.

The Coordinator taps the desktop.

Katherine stands with her feet apart and her arms folded.

The Coordinator puts down her papers.

"I won't sign anything that says I'm disabled." She speaks softly, but clearly. "I've had to go through too much to do that."

"Well, of course." She hesitates. She goes faintly red.

"I won't sign."

The Coordinator looks at the papers on her desk, then starts to flick through them. "Let me see. Let me see," she repeats. "Oh, there's an error." She looks up at Katherine. "I can get exemptions under sickness criteria for the operations and recovery period."

"I won't sign."

Her voice is more personal. "Katherine, everyone can apply under that criteria."

"Not just special students?" Her lips are dry.

"Everyone, Katherine."

"I don't know."

"Katherine, you have the right to be given the same consideration as all the other students." She stumbles over her words. "I don't regard you as different. I apologize." She stands up from behind her desk and moves towards Katherine. "I need to make the application so there is a level playing field. You've missed so much school. It's to be fair. So everyone has the same opportunity. To get entry into the college you want."

Katherine isn't sure. *I need to be a doctor, so this all makes sense.* "All right."

The Coordinator walks her to the door.

Chapter Twenty

The next weeks are tense as teachers issue assignments for the holidays, friends ask questions, Katherine sees the Professor, her mother talks about the new surgery. William's been phoning since the party. They've met a few times at Cafe Smooth with other friends. Katherine feels as though life is on hold until the operations start. She half-trains for surf-lifesaving, walks her bush track, postpones her exams. Cafe Smooth promises her regular work, but only next year.

Surgery, in a few days.

It's Saturday afternoon when William phones. "Do you need a break from studying?"

"Yes."

"Me too. Maybe we can go for a walk, then coffee and cakes afterwards? I know you like cakes, especially chocolate ones."

That makes Katherine laugh. "I'd like to, but I have to really put in some extra work before next week and you know, surgery." *I'm not hiding it anymore, not to William or anyone.*

"Does that mean you're not doing any bush walks now?"

"Well, no, but …"

"Fresh air clears the brain. I'd like to see where you go on your walks. Sounds nice."

"It is." *But I'm nervous. Another operation. It's what I want, but I'm still nervous. I can't see anyone now, especially not you, William.*

"So can I come over?"

No. "OK." She shakes her head as she puts down the receiver. *Why did I say that? I don't want to go out with William.*

"Mum. Mum." Katherine searches the house. "Where are you?" She opens the back door and sees her mother digging in the rose garden. "Mum, I'm going for a walk."

"*Per favore*, please come here, Katherine. I want to show you this. There are buds. Pink and yellow ones."

Katherine looks at the roses, then bends to smell them. "They're pretty, but no scent, Mum."

"Too early for scent." Wiping her hands on her apron, she gets up. "I have had enough gardening today."

Katherine bites her lip. "William's coming over."

Her mother is quiet for a moment. "Katherine, I know you talk sometimes with William." She picks up her garden bucket. "Come inside. I have to put on the lasagna. Rachel has a late class tonight, and she will be hungry when she gets home." She pauses. "Would you like William to come for dinner?"

Katherine doesn't answer immediately, as they climb up the back steps. "Thank you, Mum. It means a lot that you asked. But not tonight. Thank you."

Grabbing a sweater from the pile of clothes thrown onto her chair, Katherine sits on the front steps waiting for William. His old Valiant pulls up outside the house. William gets out, carefully puts on the steering lock because he's got no car insurance. Can't afford any, he says. He walks in big strides towards the house. *Your eyes look like they're smiling, William. Hazel eyes. I still love them. I can't believe I'm going out with you.*

Hiding a sheepish grin, he gives her a card and a package. "You have to open the package first."

"That's not very polite of me."

"Be wild and break the rules."

"All right. I'll be wild." She tears the paper wrapping and starts giggling. Inside the wrapping is a porky pig made of milk chocolate with a white chocolate nose and a red ribbon around its neck. "Is this supposed to be me? I should hit you for that."

"Please, be kind. You know pigs are intelligent, affectionate and ..."

"Give up, William. But it is cute." She smiles. "Very cute. Now, can I open the card?"

"It's an early 'Get Well' card."

Katherine opens the bright yellow envelope. Inside is a pig card covered in pigs with curly tails all wrapped in bandages – *Being sick is a curly problem. It needs to be straightened out.*

"That's a terrible joke." Katherine shakes her head. "Maybe it'll improve inside the card." She reads the illustrated captions aloud. *"The owner of a pig takes Piggy to the doctor. She says, 'My poor pig has lost her voice.' The Doctor looks at Piggy and starts fixing her up. 'Doctor, what are you rubbing on her?'"* Katherine looks up at William for effect. *"OINKMENT. OINKMENT!"*

They both laugh and "oinking" can be heard all the way down to Katherine's bush track.

Katherine is surprised as William identifies trees, plants, flowers and the birds that are part of the bush. "See that small brown butterfly. That one butterfly has spread nearly everywhere in the world. I guess you've just got to be persistent."

Katherine smiles. "Persistent? Are you talking about the butterfly or you?" *Or me? I feel like a brown butterfly. Flapping my wings, trying to get somewhere, but the wings are small and fragile.* "You know a lot about the bush."

"My Boy Scout days." He gives the Boy Scout salute. "I don't admit to being that to everyone. We did a lot of bushcraft and went camping a fair bit. I liked it." He stops suddenly. "Did you hear that?"

216

"What?"

"Shush." He points to leaves and brush. "See it?" There's a little pointed nose and big brown eyes peering out of the leaves. "An echidna. There are the furry spines."

"I can't believe it. I've never seen one before, except in the zoo."

"You've probably passed by echidnas before, but you haven't noticed."

"They're beautiful."

"Yes, they are."

Silently they watch the echidna, until it burrows back into the leaves. "That was special, William."

He smiles.

"I haven't been to the Falls for ages. Can we go there? It's a bit of a detour."

"That's fine."

Katherine isn't sure what they talk about, but it feels natural as they walk between the trees, bypassing a huge fallen mountain gum. Making their way across a rickety wooden bridge, they hear water. There is a small clearing which leads to the lookout. Katherine runs towards it. William follows. "Hey, slow down. What's the hurry?"

They reach the wire fence together. Looking over it, they see the waterfall. Water breaks over the cliff face, plummeting into a rock pool. Swirling foam crashes over rocks and fallen branches until it settles into the stream. Silently, they watch the water's movements. Katherine shivers.

"Are you cold? "

She nods.

"It gets cold in the late afternoon." He moves closer to her. She keeps staring down at the water crashing into the pool. He puts his arm around her. "Is that warmer?"

What are you doing? Take your arm off me. Don't you dare touch me. But you gave me a pig. I like the pig and the card. "Yes, it's warmer."

William touches her hair. "It's so soft."

Don't touch my hair. It's been pulled and dragged over scars. There are burns. Don't you remember? I'm too complicated.

He starts stroking her hair, and she wants to stop him, but it feels warm, comforting, and Katherine feels as if her body's made of clay. She half-whispers a protest. *You don't like me, do you?* Her stomach butterflies into knots and yearnings. *Stop … stop, William. Please … don't stop … don't stop.*

He turns her face to him.

You're too close, William. I'm ugly. You know it. You can see. Instinctively she raises a hand to hide scars.

He takes her hand, drawing it aside. Breathing slowly, he puts his arms around her. His breathe intermingles with hers, and gently, he kisses her lips.

Dinner, family, chatter. Katherine is quiet. She clears the table. Dishes are washed and dried and the evening routine completed. "I'm tired. I'm going to bed early. Goodnight,

Mum. Rachel."

I want to dream tonight.

Katherine opens her window to look out into the evening garden with its shadowy lights and fragrant scents. She puts the chocolate pig next to Pup on the windowsill. The cold of the night air makes her tremble as she takes off her sweater, dragging it over her head. Unbuttoning her blouse slowly, she shivers. Her jeans slide down her thighs and she rubs the small indentation the button has left on her stomach. Unclipping her bra, she watches the plain white cotton drop to the floor. She rubs the palms of her hands over the silky satin of her slip as she slides into it. Something special she bought herself for her birthday. There is no flannel nightie or pajamas tonight.

Goosebumps ripple over her body as she stands in her satin slip looking around her room. There are photographs of her mother, Rachel, Katherine; textbooks piled on her bookshelf; Pup at the window; cream for her scars; her golden necklace on her dressing table; birthday cards displayed; drawers filled with letters, medical appointments, assignments …

She puts William's card next to her bed, switches off her side lamp, then slides under the warmth of her quilt, letting sleep gradually descend.

Hands stroke her wounds, but they don't hurt her. Tingles

wander along her spine radiating into her arms and legs. Hands linger over her face and arms, before stroking her long brown hair. Hands trace the intricacies of her neck, her back, sides, body, brushing over her like wings of butterflies.

Chapter Twenty-One

"*M*um should get her promotion, don't you think? She deserves it."

"She will, Rachel. Mum can do anything."

"Mama can do anything, Rachey." Katherine lifts her chin up, watching their mother organize the tables for the lunch at the Burn Support Group in the Health Center.

Sometimes special people like firefighters talk about how to keep safe. Once Katherine and Rachel hid under the table when they were giving a parent talk about fires that sweep through towns where homes and families perished; house fires where kids were left burned and alone; the burning Twin Towers. The sisters held onto each other under the table. Afterwards, Rachel slept with her nightlight on. Katherine slept in her mother's bed for a long time, with her hand touching her mama, so that she'd never be burned again, and her mama wouldn't leave her.

The kids love the firefighters. They wear uniforms with shiny buttons and bring coloring books and stickers. Katherine is allowed to press the siren. Rachel wants to press it as well, but there are too many kids, and she's not burned. The firefighters always bring their fire truck and they are allowed to climb on board.

Once there was a special visitor, Kim Phuc, who looked beautiful. She wore a sparkling blue ai-do, and you couldn't see her burns. After her visit, their mama baked cakes for the fundraising table for the Kim Phuc Foundation that helps children of war. Their mama said, "Kim Phuc's burns made her stronger and lead others to do good." Katherine was proud that day. Rachel was quiet. She wanted to be special too.

Sometimes their mother speaks about Katherine at the meetings of the Support Group and they clap for their mama. Sometimes other parents speak, but Katherine knows they never clap for other mothers as loudly as for her mama.

While their mother is busy with lunch, Katherine and Rachel play on the swings in the playground attached to the Center. A boy who can't separate his fingers, throws a ball with his left hand to Katherine, who throws it to Rachel, who throws it to a pretty dark girl. The dark girl can't stretch her arm out properly, and the ball rolls past her. She starts to cry.

"What is wrong, mia cara? Do not cry. It cannot be so bad," Mama calls to the little girl, leaving the luncheon preparations. She hurries over. *"Do not be upset. It is only a game."* The girl's tears wiggle crookedly down her burned cheeks, and Katherine's mother wipes them gently away. *"I have special pink limonata. Lemonade. Would you like some?"* She takes the girl's hand and they go to get some pink lemonade. The girl stops crying.

"See, Mama can do anything," she tells Rachel, who's getting the ball.

Rachel picks up a magazine from the table. She hands it to Katherine. "There's a great article on rock bands in here. You can read it in the hospital."

Katherine puts the magazine in her bag. "The Professor says the operation is going to be long."

"You want this surgery, don't you?"

"Yes." Katherine puts the "Good Luck" cards everyone has given her in a pile. "I couldn't believe the Coordinator sent me a card. Have a look at this one from Jessie. It's very Jessie."

Rachel reads the front. *"Aw, C'mon! Cuddly-Wuddly Puppy wants you to cheer up!"*

She opens it.

"Kinda makes you want to squeeze cuddly-wuddly puppy's little neck until his itsy-witsy button eyes pop off, doesn't it?"

Rachel smiles. "Remind me not to get a hug from Jessie."

"Come on, Pup, into my bag." Katherine shows Rachel William's piggy card. She doesn't show her the card from their father, which says he'll visit her in the hospital.

"Ready?" her mother asks Katherine, as they begin a routine as familiar as having breakfast, but this morning there is no breakfast.

"Just be prepared. It is a long operation," her mother says, as they drive to the hospital.

"You are beautiful as you are," her mother says, as they wait for admissions.

"Your hair transplants already cover the burning, and your hair is soft and lovely," her mother says, as they go to the ward.

"I'll be perfect one day, Mum."

Tears fill her mother's eyes.

Admission. Hospital. Preparations. Nervousness. No visitors. The Professor, doctors, nurses, procedures. Her mother. Pup. "Mum, I want this."

Her mother walks beside her as the gurney is rolled along familiar corridors towards the operating room. The orderly jokes with Katherine, and her mother hovers as always, protecting her against strangers. The Professor peers over Katherine before the surgery. "Are you sure? Do you understand?"

"Yes, I'm sure. Yes, I understand," *that I'm afraid. Mama, I'm afraid.* She stretches her hands out towards her mother as the anesthetic takes effect.

"You are already perfect, my Katherine," her mother whispers, as Katherine is taken behind closed doors.

The operating team prepare, inject, monitor. Saline infiltrates Katherine's smooth, elastic skin selected for the donor site. The skin is stretched tightly, but not too tightly. The pressure is even, the cutting blade positioned as the Professor determines the depth of the cut. Slicing the skin strip to exactly the right thickness, he collects the vital skin he needs. Blood, drips, gauze, forceps … the medical team work carefully. The Professor slices tissue from her thigh, sculpting it with all the detail of an artist fashioning plaster. Katherine's face is cut open. Perspiration drips along his surgical mask as the Professor works, reinventing the side of Katherine's face.

The surgery is slow and methodical, requiring intense concentration. Exhausted from the hours of surgery, the Professor finally closes the wounds.

Recovery. Stabbing pain forces Katherine into temporary wakefulness. She opens her eyes and sees her mother sitting beside her. "Mama." She reaches for her. The nurse injects pethidine. Nausea. Katherine slips in and out of consciousness.

The days are disturbed, filled with slow recovery. Katherine doesn't even pretend to smile when the Professor checks her, but she knows. *I'll get better. The pain will go. I'm so tired of this.* She tries to turn on her side, but the stabbing pain in her head makes her gasp. *When will it end? When? I want to blame someone. Mum? Rachel? My father? Me? Who? I hate this. I can't even dream about being Beauty. I'm the Beast. I don't want to be the Beast. A Beast, beast, beast …*

🦋

Every four hours the nurse changes the fluid in the drip. Another nurse flashes her flashlight through the ward, checking patients. As her mother wets Katherine's forehead with a hand towel, she speaks to her softly, "*Bambina, bambina*, it will be over soon. Soon. Soon."

🦋

Her mother wakes up, startled by the clank of a metal bucket. "Sorry," the cleaner says, as he mops under the bed. Katherine opens her eyes, then closes them. The hospital routine irritates her today. She turns away from her mother when she speaks to her and pretends to be asleep when the nurse comes in. Rachel calls, and her mother speaks to her, but Katherine doesn't want to talk. She rolls onto her side and watches the morning drag into midday, then afternoon.

The Professor and his team arrive in the late afternoon. "How are you, Katherine?"

"Better. I've been waiting," she stammers.

Her mother is waiting too.

The Professor nods. "I expect you're nervous, Katherine. But we have to give some time for healing to start."

I just want to know. I don't want to wait anymore. I've been waiting all my life. "Has it worked?"

"I hope so, Katherine." He explains the technical details of the operation to the students as he carefully unbandages a small section. The Professor flushes slightly. He takes a deep breath. "All right, let's see."

The Professor's team watches expectantly. Katherine and her mother wait expectantly. Katherine's mother squeezes her daughter's hand. As the Professor bends his head, all they can see is his thinning white hair. Then he looks up. "It's taking, but we'll know more in a few days."

"Can I see it? Can I?"

"Not yet. Not until we take off the bandages. No congratulations until then. You take it easy until those bandages are off."

"I will. I will."

Katherine's mother goes back to work. She doesn't get her promotion. "You took off too much time," they say. "We need someone more reliable."

Every afternoon, her mother and Rachel visit Katherine. Jessie comes twice. Then one morning, there is a man at the end of her bed. He's got reddish hair and is tall. Katherine only half-recognizes her father at first. He hands her a large box of chocolates. "How are you?"

She takes the chocolates. A sense of another time overtakes her. *Is this unfinished business? Am I three again? Is that you visiting when Mum is out of the room? Rachel was so angry at you.*

"Did the operation work out, Katherine?"

"I'm not sure. Maybe." There's silence.

His shifts uncomfortably at the foot of the bed. "So, I hope you're feeling all right."

"I'm all right." *I am, you know. Mum, Rachel and me. We're all right.* "I'm glad we met in the cafe."

"I am too."

"The flowers for my birthday were nice. Pink roses." There's a long silence. "Mum grows roses. They're lovely." *Your pink roses died, and I had to throw them out. Mum's roses are there all year — stalks, new leaves, buds. They're always there for me. Mum's there's for me.*

"Your mother was always a great gardener."

"She works at it. You have to take care of a garden, if it's going to grow." *You didn't take care of me and help me grow, did you?* "Thanks for coming to visit." Katherine looks at him. *You don't drink now, and you're sorry, but I can't give you anything. Not now, maybe not ever. I'm glad you like where you live and what you do. A geologist in the outback. But it has nothing to do with me.* "If you want to call me, it's all right sometimes, and send a card. I'd like a card." She waits for a moment. "But I don't want you to visit the hospital again. It'd hurt Mum and Rachel," *and they're too important to me.*

He stands there not saying anything. When the tea lady arrives, Katherine turns away from him and asks for coffee and cookies.

"Well, I better go then."

"Yes. Thanks for the chocolates." *I'm glad you visited. I*

needed to see you. Now I need you to leave.

Tomorrow is the day. Bandages off. Katherine tries to sleep, but she calls out in her dreams. The nurse flashes a light over Katherine's bed, startling her.

"Sorry if I frightened you. Are you all right?"

"What time is it?"

"Three in the morning. Get some sleep."

When she opens her eyes it's suddenly six, and the hospital is alive and busy – blood pressures taken, pills distributed, cleaners mopping floors, breakfast trays. Her mother arrives. "I want to make sure I am here before the Professor comes." She drops her handbag on the bed. "You look tired, Katherine. You did not sleep well last night?" She's brought the first rose of the season. The rose petals are pink and smooth.

"I slept fine, Mum."

"I will find a vase."

The Professor is much earlier than usual. He's accompanied by a large group of doctors. Katherine's mother follows them into the room with the vase.

"So it's time, Katherine. Are you ready?"

She presses her hands hard against the mattress. "Yes, I'm ready."

He chats with her about surfing, school, what she plans for the holidays, as he unwraps the bandages. Katherine tries to listen, tries to answer. The final bandage is removed. Katherine's mother gasps. There is excited talk among the doctors. "Remember, there's a lot of swelling, but it will settle

229

down. There'll need to be more work done on it too." The Professor rubs his chin.

Taking a deep breathe, she asks, "Can I wear my hair up?"

"Not yet. There are a few more things to do first, but I hope one day."

I will wear my hair up. "Thank you. Thank you."

The doctors leave, talking about the surgery. "Mum, Mum, get your mirror. I want to see. I want to see." She riffles through her mother's handbag. "I can't wait. Where's the mirror? Where? Got it." The morning sunlight hits the glass as she flips open the mirror case. "It's too bright." She turns her back to the sunlight. "I'm going to be normal like you always said. Beautiful, maybe even perfect."

She lifts her long hair away from her face, pulling it so that it hangs down on her left side. Then she holds the mirror so that it reflects the side of her face. She holds the mirror very still. Very still. From her red, distorted skin, there is a thick, pulpy mass like an old eraser glued onto the side of her head. Red and misshapen. Like an alien growth.

Katherine stares questioningly at her mother. "You said I would be beautiful. You said that. You lied to me." She throws the mirror onto the floor. It crashes into a myriad of splinters.

"You lied. Lied."

Katherine sobs in her mother's arms.

Chapter Twenty-Two

*S*he doesn't dream of Beasts and Beauties. She doesn't dream at all, but the nights are frightening. V.V. Sipos' lines chant like nightmares, "the hiders, hunching their shoulder, huddled in obscurity." In the morning, she's exhausted.

"I'm sorry, Mum. You'd never lie to me." "Yes, I think everything is going to be great, Professor." "Rachel, my face is still swollen. I don't want to show anyone." "William, call every day. Don't visit." "Yes, William, afterwards I'll go with you to a basketball game." "No, I can't see you yet, but soon, Jessie." "No visitors, except Mama."

What's wrong with me, Pup? I expected something different. Looking into the mirror. She shudders. *It was the shock, that's all. The Professor said it was too early to see. Hey Pup, tell me to shut up. I've got to get myself together. You know, Pup …* She touches his bald old head. *Your ears are a bit hairy. At least I'll never have hairy ears. But you wait, one day … I was disappointed. Isn't that a pathetic word? Disappointment. I've had a lot of that. But you know what? I'm not going to hide. I've got Mum and Rachel. I can't hide, not after everything I've been through. But I want to hide. I do.*

Every day she escapes into the bathroom to look in the mirror. She gasps, leaning on the white porcelain basin with its stainless steel faucet. Her hair falls like tangled string down her back, but she can't bear to comb it. When Rachel visits, she sits by Katherine's bed and gently teases out the knots, brushing and brushing, making her sister's hair shine.

As Katherine lifts up her hair and looks into the mirror, she catches her breath. *I think the swelling is less. Is it getting better? I think it is.*

Every day, the swelling reduces a little more. *Please, please, let it get better.* Every day it looks a little less red, less alien. *Maybe the Professor's right. It needs time.* Then one day, her face starts to look like hers. Katherine stares motionless into the mirror. *Are you part of me? Is that my skin? No, you're still red, imperfect.* Katherine nervously touches her face, edging her fingers carefully under her hair, over her ear. *I'm scared.* She traces her face with the tip of her finger, then with all her

232

fingers. It's still swollen, but better. Katherine smiles.

"There will be more surgery, Katherine. You'll be in and out of the hospital, Katherine," the Professor says.

Katherine closes her hands tightly. *It looks better and maybe ... beautiful. One day. Just a few more months. By the end of the year, it'll be better. By Christmas, it'll be better.*

When Katherine arrives home from the hospital, Rachel is waiting at the front door. "I'm back." Katherine smiles.

"Does that mean you'll keep the bathroom tidy?" Rachel teases. "I know that's impossible." She hugs her sister. "I missed you."

"Me too."

Their mother walks behind Katherine with her bag. "It's good you're home." She puts down the bag and heads for the kitchen. "We will have tea first. We are all tired."

The kettle boiling, they settle in the family room. Sunlight filters through the windows. Emotions dissipate, and there's disbelief that the hospital is over.

Rachel pours the tea, then sits down. "So, Katherine, when do I see it?"

"Remember, my face is still swollen, but it's improving." Katherine breathes deeply as she pulls back her hair.

Her mother and sister look at each other, then Katherine. "It's better."

Katherine smiles. "It's better."

The phone rings. It's Nonna. Their mother picks up the receiver. Katherine nestles into her armchair enjoying the ebb and flow of her mother's words. "Katherine," "surgery," "Professor," "surgery," "bandages"… until tears dot the corners of her mother's eyes, until she's smiling, until she says, "Katherine is home now."

Rachel walks out of the room before she hears her mother add, "And Rachel."

Her mother takes the phone to Katherine. "*Cara Bambina*, Katherine. It is very good about your operation. We will see you soon at Christmas. Autumn is starting, and the leaves of the oak trees are yellow and lovely, but it is cold. There is snow in the mountains."

"I promise it'll be hot here. You and Grandpapa can swim."

"Yes, Grandpapa enjoys swimming. Ah, was it good, the sweater I knitted for you to keep you warm in the hospital?"

"The bed jacket? Oh, yes, it was really warm, Nonna," *stuffed at the back of my cupboard.*

Grandpapa takes the phone, but his English isn't very good, and he speaks disjointedly about the fishermen and big catches. He doesn't take his boat out so much anymore, and there is loss in his voice for the passing of a part of his life. Katherine sympathizes, but it seems so far away. Her mother takes back the phone to speak to Grandpapa. As a girl, she went with her father on fishing expeditions into the Mediterranean Sea. She talks to him as though it's still her home. She always finds it hard to say goodbye to her parents.

She sits in another armchair near Katherine.

"Mama, you love Italy." Her mother nods. "I've wondered,

why didn't you go back to Italy after my father left? When I've asked before, you never answered. Didn't Nonna and Grandpapa want you back?"

She reflects for a while, then looks at Katherine. "It's difficult to think about, but I have nothing to hide. Your Nonna and Grandpapa wanted me to go home. They had forgiven me."

"So why did you stay here?"

She hesitates. "My pride. When I left my college in the middle of my studying and ran away with my handsome foreigner, I told my parents that they knew nothing." Her lips tremble a little. "I was the one who knew nothing."

"Then you were burned, and there was so much to do. I had to be in a big city for the doctors, the hospitals. There were no such hospitals in the village."

"It's been hard here, Mum."

"Yes, but here is where we live. You have grown up here. Our life is here." She leans towards Katherine and gently kisses her check.

"Thank you for telling me."

Katherine goes to her room, unpacks, puts Pup on his shelf, turns on her music and lies on her bed. She closes her eyes, glad to be lying on her own bed, glad that her mother and sister are in the house. William is coming over tonight. Her stomach flutters. *Is it too soon? My scars?* She can't wear her hair up or bouncing in a ponytail like Jessie does. But one day.

She wakes up with a jerk. It's the afternoon already, and

William's taking her to a basketball game. It's panic – shower, hair, clothes. What to wear? "Rachel, Rachel, I need your help. Do I look all right in this?" Katherine's banging on Rachel's bedroom door.

Rachel looks up. Katherine is wearing her blue jeans and black top with colored diamantes. The red, blue, clear crystals sparkle, matching her shoes. Her hair waves down to her shoulders. "You look good."

"Do I? Do I?"

Rachel nods.

"You're the best sister." Katherine doesn't notice Rachel look down. As Katherine runs out the door, Rachel whispers, "I hope Liz's brother phones soon."

There's the sound of a horn beeping. "That's William. Got to go," she calls out to her mum and sister.

The Valiant has been waxed and polished and sparkles in places. In other places no amount of waxing and polishing can help. The chrome bumper bar is tied on with rope so that it doesn't fall off. William plans to work on the car, doing a few essential repairs, like fixing the leaking radiator and spluttering carburetor. "Your car looks terrific," Katherine says, as she jumps in.

"It'll sound terrific too, after I've worked on it this weekend."

There are no difficult silences. All their talking on the phone has made them comfortable with each other. He asks about her surgery.

"It'll be perfect by Christmas." *Perfect? As perfect as it can be, and then I'll have to accept whatever I am.* She brushes her hand over William's.

They chat about the pressure of exams for a while, then they talk about surfing and the basketball game tonight. "Do you mind going to the Club after the game?" William adds, "Jessie and Greg are coming,"

"I know. Jessie already called me. Jessie said Greg's playing tonight."

"He's made it into the A's, which is great," William says. "Marc's playing as well."

Marc? "As long as it's not too late, it'll be fine to go." Marc. *Paper bag girl. It doesn't even hurt now. And this girl will have a real face. Not perfect, but better. Won't need a paper bag, but that doesn't even matter because guess what? William kissed me. No paper bag required.* Katherine settles back in the roomy car seat with its frayed edges. "These old seats are very comfortable."

Katherine looks out of the window as William drives alongside the bushland reserve. "I'm going to start running on the track again. I need to be in shape for the lifesaving season, and I like the run anyway." A tingle shivers down her back, and she folds her arms around herself. "Maybe I'll notice the echidnas this time."

William puts on a Beach Boys compilation. "Surfin' USA," "California Girls," "Rhonda"…

"You're really an old surfer, I can hear that." She hides a

smile behind her hand.

"Hey, are you laughing at me?"

"I wouldn't do that. Aren't those songs from the '60s and '70s?"

"They sure are. The Beach Boys and their clones do a few new songs occasionally these days, but I like their early music. It's what surfing is about. Riding the waves, parties, having mates, girls and a good time. Aren't you sick of the deep and meaningful stuff that's on the radio?"

"I like meaningful sometimes. I mind self-pity."

William swerves around a corner.

"I can't listen to self-pity. Yes, there's pollution, war, family breakups or whatever. But you can't just blame your parents, teachers, the government, whoever. Do something yourself." Katherine rocks in time with "Surfin' Safari."

You have to believe in yourself. Change what you're able to change, but accept what you are. No blame.

The Sports Complex is crowded with basketball players, coaches, spectators, kids running around with ice cream. The microphone blares directions for teams to get ready. Katherine sees Jessie waving at them. Motioning them to come up into the stands. She's wearing Greg's team's colors. Red ribbons in her hair and a red T-shirt. "I wonder who you support," Katherine teases.

"You're looking great." Jessie presses her hand.

Katherine smiles.

There's the whistle. The game begins. The referee tosses

the ball into the air. Marc grabs the ball, beating the Blue center to it. Throwing, dribbling, defending the ball fast and furious. Greg shoots for a basket. He gets it in. Jessie out-screams the other supporters cheering on the sidelines. The Blues have the ball now, and it's traveling fast up the court to their basket. A Blue player barges into Marc, who falls. The referee blows his whistle hard. "Foul," he calls out. Marc gets a free throw. He throws it to Greg who dribbles it fast down the court. Then a high jump shot. Another basket. The Reds are fast. The Blues can't compete against the high-speed offensive attack. Another basket. They come back with a strong defense …

Halftime. Greg leans against the railing, breathing heavily. His face is red, like his hair. Marc keeps moving with barely controlled energy. T-shirts are stained with sweat. Water from plastic bottles drips down faces. The coaches are in separate corners, directing new strategies, identifying opposition weaknesses. The concentration is intense.

Halftime's over. A Blue player passes the ball to a teammate. Marc intercepts, steals the ball, dribbling it up the court, then a Blue … Red … Blue battling …. up and down … a fury of movement and energy. The Red team defend fiercely. The Blues can't get the ball past. The Blue forward isn't as successful, and the ball travels past him. Score for Reds. Score for Blues. Score for Reds. Score for Reds. Cheering … cheering … cheering …

The Reds win with a final score of 52-38. There are the obligatory congratulations from the Blue team, but they aren't happy. In front of everyone, the Blue coach verbally attacks the center. "You didn't concentrate. Can't you play? You let the team down. You … You …" Katherine looks away because she doesn't want to see it. The Blue center is flushed with humiliation. Katherine shudders. *Coach, it's not the center who's let the team down. It's you. You're making him feel like nothing. How can he do anything then?*

William takes Katherine's hand. "Great game."

"Great game." Her swimming coach flits into her thoughts. "I'm glad we're supporting the Reds."

Jessie can't stop talking about the game until Katherine gives up. "Yes, we now know Greg is the best basketball player of all time."

"Very funny." But nothing can deflate Jessie's good mood.

They wait for Greg and Marc to come out of the locker rooms. They leave the Sports Complex together. Greg has his arm around Jessie as they cross the road and walk to the strip of small shops. Marc's meeting a few friends. William's still holding Katherine's hand. The small shops are closed except for the laundromat with its glaring light. Washing machines whirl in their cleaning cycle while two men wait inside at separate ends of the laundromat. Katherine holds William's hand tighter. *They seem so alone. I've got so much, haven't I?*

They arrive at the club. People spread out onto the sidewalk. They squeeze in between girls in black and guys in jeans. They see Jessie and push their way towards her. Jessie's engrossed in Greg, who's retelling every move on the basketball court. Katherine smiles and listens for a while. Marc's there with his mates. *You've changed. I can't believe it was really you who told me to hide. That no one could love me. You wouldn't now, would you? We're friends.* "Saturday will be my last game," Marc says. "After that it's studying. Final exams."

"There won't be many nights out for any of us for a while," Jessie admits.

"Can't wait till it's all over, and I get more time with you, Jessie," Greg says, under his breath. Then he laughs. "We've nearly done thirteen years at school. That's a life sentence."

"The formal will be one great party to celebrate." William looks at Katherine.

Marc smiles at Katherine. "I'm ready to go. Anyone else coming?" A few stay on, but Greg and Jessie make their way outside. William and Katherine follow.

The old Valiant is waiting for them in the parking lot. Katherine pretends to hug it, making William laugh. In the car, William puts on the radio. They both smile when a surfing song comes on as he drives Katherine home.

"I guess we'll both be busy for the next few months, William."

"We probably won't have a chance to see as much of each other for a while." He hesitates. "I may as well ask you now. Would you like to come with me to my formal?"

The surfing song echoes through the car.

... do you love me?
come on, come on, come on,
surfin' girl.

He glances at her. "I couldn't take anyone else."

surfin' girl
I love the way you walk
I love the way you talk.

Hazel eyes. *I knew I always loved them.*

do you love me?
do you surfin' girl?
I love you.

"Yes, I'd like to go to the formal with you, William."

Chapter Twenty-Three

The next months are like colored confetti at a wedding. Bits and pieces of school, Rachel, surf-lifesaving, her mother, friends, William, float fragmented over the hospital with its veil of surgery.

The garden blooms in the warmth of summer. Butterflies flutter browns and blues between roses. Only the worn paling fence separates the spread of color. Birds of paradise, kangaroo paw, pink roses, marigolds spread from the porch right to the back fence, meeting the dusty green bush. Rosellas peck at the baskets of seeds hanging on the gums.

Katherine and Jessie lie under the trees on a checkered blanket. They drink water from bottles. It's hot, and they pick at the grass. "Greg came for dinner last week. Dad sort of approves of him because Greg plans to be a lawyer. Mum just wants peace and quiet, so she likes anyone." Jessie rolls onto her back. "But what matters is that I really like him, and it's not all one-way. He's asks me about who I am. He's coming with me to the new science exhibition at the Powerhouse Museum."

Katherine smiles. "That's good, because it did look one-way."

"It's two-way now." Jessie's blonde hair glistens in the afternoon sun, and her eyes are tender as she tells her friend about midnight walks, and how he caught her when she tripped. "His hands touched me and ..."

William's touched my face. Kissed me. I loved his hands stroking my hair, but when he touched my shoulder, my arms, there were scars. How can he touch me?

There are more grafts on the side of her face, more redefining. Katherine misses school. *I'm nearly there.* The teachers send assignments. *I'm nearly there. Just.* The Coordinator gets a time extension for the completion of the university entrance exam. *I'm nearly there.* Nausea and recovery. *Nearly there. Nearly.*

The back doors are open, letting the late spring breeze filter through the house. Dressed in a black dinner suit and a plain white silk shirt, William sits in a chair, waiting. Katherine's mother hands him a small box. "She will be here soon."

Rachel does last minute touches to Katherine's hair. She

threads a thin blue ribbon through it.

"Can you see the operations?"

"You look pretty, Katherine."

"But there're still scars." *I'm scared. Why am I always scared inside?*

"Go on. William's waiting."

Katherine looks at her sister. "I love you, Rachel." She takes a breath, glances at Rachel, then opens her bedroom door. William is holding a white gardenia. He looks up as she walks into the room. She smiles at him.

He smiles too.

The satin of her pale blue dress shimmers in the evening light. Nervously, she touches her gold necklace with its three tiny diamonds. Katherine's hair is half swept up.

He moves towards her and hands her the gardenia. Katherine ties it around her wrist. "It's lovely."

He hands her a small box. "Your mother wanted me to give you this."

She unwraps it slowly. There is some tissue paper inside. Opening the paper, she sees them. *I can't believe it. They're so beautiful.*

William strokes her face. She wants to move backwards, but doesn't. The small earrings match her necklace. They sparkle as he slides them onto her ears.

The days are busy with preparations for a traditional Christmas.

The turkey is stuffed, vegetables peeled, sliced and ready for the oven. The ham is in the fridge. It only has to be cut up and the fresh mangoes, pineapples and fruit displayed around it. King-size prawns and oysters have been bought and the sauces made. The fridge is overflowing. Italian specialties are part of it too, with little plates of ravioli, scallops, olives. The favorite is panettone, sweet cake filled with candied fruit, it has been baked and sits cooling on the kitchen table.

The house is festive. The sun beats down on the front window stenciled with snowflakes and a large white Santa. Christmas cards line the mantelpiece. The Professor's card takes pride of place in the center. The fir tree is decorated with tinsel and baubles. Presents are piled under its branches.

Christmas Eve. Nonna arrives wearing thick stockings, boots and a woolen dress. Grandpapa wears an open shirt and jacket. There is hugging and kissing, and their mother cries at the airport.

Nonna and their mother talk all the way home. When they arrive at the house, their mother has to show them everything – her house, garden, the birds that visit, the bush that surrounds them. Then there are photo albums. They pour over the years. Katherine and Rachel before the accident, the burns, hospital, doctors, the Professor, picnics, the elastic suit and yellow sausage, school, friends, operations … Nonna and Grandpapa ask to see how Katherine looks now, with her hair swept up.

She pulls back her hair, exposing her neck, her face.

"*Bene*, Katherine." "*Bella*, Katherine." They nod, but Katherine can see they only partially understand that it is really wonderful.

Her mother is smiling. *You understand totally, don't you, Mama?*

Jet lag finally catches up with them, and Nonna and Grandpapa go to sleep in Rachel's room. Rachel likes her work. Talks to Jill a lot. She's got a double date. Liz's brother called. She didn't want to move in with Katherine.

"You just have to accept it. Maybe you'll learn to be messy like me. You're lucky. I'm listening to the Beach Boys now," Katherine's voice tinkled.

Rachel didn't laugh. Her mother bought a fold up bed for Katherine's room.

On Christmas morning, Nonna is wearing a cotton shift, and she's changed her heavy boots for sandals. Grandpapa has already gone local and is wearing shorts, a T-shirt and running shoes. Christmas carols play in the background as they sit around the tree to give and receive presents. Katherine gives her mother and Rachel their favorite perfumes, but the gifts seem trivial. *Nothing could ever compare to what I've got already.* There are presents of clothing, soaps, diaries, sweets and money from Grandpapa and Nonna.

At Christmas lunch, Grandpapa carves the turkey. Katherine can't remember anyone except her mother doing that. Grandpapa makes jokes in broken English. Katherine laughs, even though she only half-understands them. Their mother and Nonna laugh. There is wine at the table, but Grandpapa drinks a beer. There has never been beer in their house before. Grandpapa holds Nonna's hand and calls her *Cara*, but he calls Rachel, *Principessa*, Princess. And Katherine, *Bellezza*, Beauty.

The women clear the table, wash dishes, stack leftovers in the fridge. Nonna and Rachel take charge of tidying the family room with its wrapping paper and gifts. Nonna asks about Rachel's work and her friends and if she has a boyfriend. Rachel stares at the carpet. No one really asks about Rachel. It's always been looking after Katherine. Suddenly, she's crying. Nonna takes her hand. They walk into the garden. "I want to know you, Rachel."

In the late afternoon, William drives up in his Valiant. Grandpapa is very interested in the car and looks under the hood with him. His broken English doesn't seem to matter when they discover they both love the sea. They talk about big seas and currents and the vagaries of the ocean.

It's early evening by the time William and Katherine get the chance to walk in the garden together. "I hope you like this present."

He unwraps the surfing book. "Katherine. You know me. Thanks."

She shakes her head when she opens the Beach Boys CD he's bought her. There is another package with it. "What's in this? I bet it's sand."

"No, you lose that bet."

She opens the box. The silver charm bracelet tinkles in her hands. Taking it from her, William clasps it around her wrist. Slowly, he runs his hand up her arm, drawing her to him.

"I know your burns are part of you. That makes them OK."

I want to be perfect. I'm not, am I? Even after all the surgery. Doesn't it matter, William? Do you really mean that?

He pushes her hair away from her face and kisses her gently.

From her bedroom window, Katherine sees kookaburras on the clothesline. She sees her mother's roses and smells the scents of the bush. Butterflies defy their fragile wings and dance in the breeze, *like me.*

She turns to look at Rachel, who is sound asleep. She's become close with Nonna. Katherine feels a twinge of jealousy, but shakes it away. Pup is on Katherine's bed. *I can't explain how much I love you, Mum, Rachel. I'm lucky there are so many people in my life. The Professor and everyone in the hospital. Jessie and Liz, my school friends, Mr. Roberts, even the Coordinator. There's William. I think I love him. And Nonna and Grandpapa are here.*

I've got things I want to do. Lifesaving. Championships, I hope. Work at Cafe Smooth. That'll give me money for vacation. Study hard. I'm going to be a doctor. I just know it. She wipes away tears. *Why am I crying? Professor, I'm going to be a hero like you.*

There'll always be some scars but I'm not so scared anymore.
I don't feel like the Beast anymore.
Not now.
Not ever.

Butterflies

Every survivor has a story. Often the story is of interest, and even more often, instructive. "Butterflies" is the story of a burn survivor, and is both interesting and instructive. It explores the complex areas of the emotional impact of a burn on the individual and family while giving insight into the world of hospitals, patients and doctors. It traces the development of the personality from insecurity and relative isolation to a healthier level of self-esteem that enables the individual to form balanced relationships with family and friends. It shows how the inner person can triumph over a preoccupation with surface scars, and know that basic values of commitment, caring and trust are more important than the texture of the skin.

"Butterflies" has relevance outside the narrow circle of burn survivors and their families. It shows the ebb and flow of emotions that affect us all, particularly in the transition between childhood and adulthood, and how parenting and family life make these bearable.

Those of us who are involved in the world of burns know how survivors need help from time to time, but slowly develop a depth of character and an inner strength which is rarely seen in others. Like tempering steel, the process of passing through the fire helps make a person of exceptional quality. "Butterflies" captures these subtleties for the reader, and gives a stunning insight into a difficult topic.

Dr. Hugh Martin, O.A.M.
President of the Australian and New Zealand Burn Association and Head of the Burn Unit, The Children's Hospital at Westmead, Sydney.

About the Author

The daughter of Hungarian refugees, Susanne Gervay is the mother of two children. A lecturer, educational consultant, and award-winning author, she has been recognized for her writing on social justice for young people. Her story "Days of Thailand" in the anthology "Fear Factor: Terror Incognito" sits alongside Sir Salman Rushdie, David Malouf, and Thomas Keneally. Her story "To East Timor" in the IBBY, UNICEF anthology "Peace Story" is one of 22 youth stories written for peace from 22 counties including the USA, Uganda, Korea, and Japan.

Susanne's "Jack" books are rite-of-passage Australian fiction, translated into numerous languages. She is recognized for her light touch, blending humor and issues into accessible narratives reaching both young people and adults. "I Am Jack" on school bullying, adapted into a play by premiere theater company Monkey Baa, continues to tour theaters each year.

Susanne's books are endorsed by significant organizations including Room to Read, the Children's Hospital Sydney, and the Cancer Council Australia, which gave their yellow daffodil logo to her "Always Jack."

An international festival speaker, she is also co-head of the SCBWI Australia & New Zealand, sits on the board of the Writers Centre and served as Australia Day Ambassador. She's been awarded the University of Technology Sydney Outstanding Professional Achievement Award and received the Lady Cutler Award for Distinguished Services to Children's Literature.

www.sgervay.com